Current Disasters

Short fiction
By Jen McConnell

ROADSIDE PRESS

Editor: Michele McDannold
Original cover art: Ned McConnell
Cover design: Sam Hanna
Author photo: Nikia Reveal

Roadside Press
Colchester, Illinois

Table of Contents

For Dan, as ever

Last Bus to Stonehenge

Bad traffic added time to the bus ride so when Penny stepped off in Levi's Plaza, the street was empty. Penny closed her eyes and breathed in the mist and briny smell of the bay. She could feel, ever so slightly, the vibrations of past lives around her. This area of San Francisco had been built up, burned down, and rebuilt so many times, remaking but not erasing its history.

The theater door opened as Penny reached for it. She walked into the musty lobby where an usher raised her cane to block the path.

"It's already started."

"I'm sorry but please," Penny said. "It would be a shame not to support the show."

The usher grumbled but took Penny's ticket and led her into the darkness, stopping at a seat on the aisle. Penny couldn't see anything but felt the closeness of the audience. She shivered, remembering the theater was once an icehouse.

Unable to read the playbill in the dark, she had no warning that, when the spotlight came on, the stocky, dark-haired man standing alone on stage wore nothing but socks and black shoes.

Penny didn't know what to do. She tried not to stare at the naked man but there wasn't anything else on stage but a hard-backed chair. Maybe it was a joke to make a fool of the audience, an absurdist play to see who would laugh first.

A citrusy scent, maybe from perfume or an air freshener, clogged her senses, making her lightheaded. When the other character, a woman named Emma, walked on stage fully clothed, she didn't seem to notice the man's nakedness. Penny waited for them to acknowledge it but they didn't and after the third scene, she slipped out of her seat, leaving her program behind. The usher called after Penny as she burst through the door into the chilly night.

On the bus to her apartment, Penny felt prudish to be that embarrassed by a man's nudity. She found the play, *Last Bus to Stonehenge*, on her phone and bought a ticket for the next night's performance.

Penny didn't invite anyone to join her. She wasn't close to her coworkers. She heard them go to lunch in various pairs and trios, but after she turned them down a few times, they stopped asking. Working with them on projects was fine but manufacturing small talk was exhausting. With her few friends, she had regular activities: movies with Lauren, Sunday yoga with Melissa. She joined Rebecca, her cousin in the East Bay, for flea markets and concerts. Rebecca also invited Penny to spend every holiday at her house and sometimes Penny accepted.

After a quick nod at a different usher on Friday night, Penny was surprised to find herself seated in the front row. She must have turned the room around in her head when she bought the ticket. She consulted the program—the play had three acts, one location, and two characters: Pedro and Emma.

When the spotlight came up on Pedro, he stood still, waiting, like there was no one else in the theater. The middle-aged man seated next to Penny said, "You've got to be kidding me," and stood up. He reached for the hand of his date, who was staring at Pedro. She glanced over at Penny before taking the man's hand. Penny heard laughter from the crowd as they left. When Pedro began to speak, Penny felt a strange energy, like buzzing from a neon sign, and tried to remember the last time she saw a man naked.

Her last date didn't get that far. Lauren had set Penny up with a finance guy, Colin, she knew from work. They decided to go out to dinner and if that went well, see a movie. He made reservations at a fusion restaurant in Pac Heights and ordered a bottle of wine without asking what Penny liked. After she ordered her meal, Colin asked the server to pick his meal for him.

"Surprise me," he said.

Penny was embarrassed for him but wasn't sure why.

"I'll eat anything," Colin said, after approving the wine Penny knew she wouldn't like.

"But don't you know what you want?"

"I know what I want," he said, "but I don't know what I don't know, see? If I always eat the same thing, how will I ever try anything new?"

Penny couldn't disagree but was still put off by Colin's garrulous manner—talking so much but saying nothing. As he paid the check, waving away Penny's offer to split it, she said that she felt a migraine coming on, perhaps from the tannins in the wine, and was going home. That was the end of Colin.

At the first scene change, Penny left her seat. She was too close, too exposed, to Pedro's nakedness to feel comfortable. Seeking refuge in the empty lobby, she wondered who was naked: the actor or the character. It would be different if Pedro was clothed and the other characters pretended he was naked. Or they were all naked. Penny stepped outside, confused, feeling the air cool down her flushed face.

She shivered as she waited for the bus, imagining going to the show with Colin. He'd probably whisper throughout the play, explaining the subtext to her. She opened the phone app and purchased a ticket for Saturday night, making sure it wasn't in the front row, so she could ignore Pedro and give the story her full attention.

"You're here again." It was a statement, not a question, from the usher who was there the first night. "Staying for the whole play this time?"

Penny blushed. "Had an emergency."

"Sure, honey," the woman said as Penny disappeared into the nearly full theater.

She scooted past a few people to reach the center seat of the middle row. There was a different energy emanating from that spot, like when a plane begins to descend. She yawned to pop her ears. She thumbed through her well-worn program to read the description of the theater again. It was built with extra-thick walls and floors that sloped slightly toward the center to let the melting ice drain into the ground beneath. The drain had been—maybe it still was—right under her seat.

This time, Penny concentrated on Pedro's face so she could follow the story. Pedro was from Mexico and Emma was from Texas. They were vacationing in England and now arguing about visiting Stonehenge on their last day. Emma had dreamed of seeing Stonehenge since she'd first played princess and dragons. Pedro was sure she'd be disappointed.

"Remember Big Ben," he said. "We waited in line for so long. And for what?"

"But Stonehenge is an energy vortex—"

"Not this again."

"It's a convergence of all ley lines around the world. They say the area has healing powers. Just by being there. Like the pyramids in Egypt and the Mayan ruins in Mexico."

"But you never want to go to Mexico, do you?" Pedro asked.

Penny's thoughts drifted to an article she read dismissing the idea of ley lines and energy vortexes. The writer didn't call them hoaxes exactly but implied people who believed in them were gullible at best and stupid at worst. An old Vermont hippie was quoted as saying that ley lines were what humans—and in turn, the earth—inherited and passed on when connections were made between people, over time, through experiences. Penny didn't understand how someone could disagree that different places had different energy.

She spent so much time thinking about Stonehenge and ley lines that the curtain had come down before she focused back in. As the audience clapped, Penny took out her phone and bought a ticket to the next day's final performance.

For the matinee, Penny's seat was in the back row. Here it felt cold, a dead spot, a draft from the emergency exit off to her right. She imagined the old workers heaving giant blocks of ice onto the carriages in the alley, and feeding ice chips to overheated horses.

"We'll go to Mexico next," Emma was saying on stage, "but let's go to Stonehenge today."

"Do you think we can catch the last bus?" Pedro asked.

"If we hurry," Emma said. "Just let me get ready." She pulled off her white T-shirt, used it to wipe off her bright pink lipstick, and dropped it to the floor. Then she took off her jeans. As she reached back to unhook her bra, the stage lights dimmed.

Penny gasped and looked around. She caught a man's eye before he turned and whispered to the man next to him. The curtain lowered and the audience clapped. Penny stood up but didn't clap. She wanted to rush into the street, grab the first person she saw, and shout, *let me tell you about what I just saw*.

When the house lights were raised, the actors came out wearing robes. They were joined on stage by the director for a question-and-answer session. Penny left before the first question was asked. She didn't know much about art but she knew she didn't want to hear it explained. Not by Colin, not by the director.

Outside in the cold and dark, the city felt alive. Penny was bursting with thoughts and feelings—about the play's structure, nakedness, energy vortexes—but there wasn't anyone on the street to talk to. She walked past the bus stop, feeling like she did when she first moved there. Like everything was possible.

The next time she had a date, they would go to a museum or a play or a poetry reading. Any kind of art, she thought, would give the evening meaning and their conversation substance and leave her feeling something, rather than nothing, even if she went home alone at the end of night.

The Wrong Way

Of course, I thought, as the car slammed into me because I'd stepped into the road looking the wrong way. Why else would I have spent the last few weeks purging the boxes of old journals and scrapbooks and love letters if I hadn't seen the end coming. It wasn't your burden to go through my memories and I didn't want you to see that I wasn't everything you hoped I was.

The Best One-Armed Waiter in the West

On our first date, Shelly admitted she hadn't noticed right away that I only had one arm. To be fair, I was a zombie at the time.

"Zombies first," she said.

We were in line for coffee during a break on the first day of the movie shoot. She was one of the cute young villagers that wouldn't make it to the end. But I didn't know that when we met. All I knew was that female extras rarely talked to the undead.

"I haven't seen you before," I said. "Is *Stabby Stabby, Death Death* your first horror film?"

She laughed. "I'm starting to fear that's not just the working title."

"I guess Hollywood ran out of words."

"This isn't just my first horror film. It's my first film. Like, ever. I don't even know where to sit."

I stared at her as she tilted her head back to drink. The sun lit up her marble-green eyes. I'd been kicked in the teeth enough times not to get my hopes up, but it couldn't hurt to be friendly.

"Over here," I said. All the tables in the shade were taken so I led her to the edge of the forest where Zed, the lead zombie, would later gather his army. My makeup was melting into my eyes. Not that it mattered. On set was the one place where the worse I looked, the better I looked. I wiped my forehead with the back of my hand. At the table, I angled to sit on her left side. From experience, I knew the longer we went without her noticing my missing arm, the longer she would talk to me.

"My non-zombie name is Vic," I said.

"I'm Shelly. So what's your zombie name?"

"In the script, I'm number 22 but really it's 'Ahhhh' or 'Nooooo.' Whatever they scream as they run away from me."

"Do you do this often?" she asked. "Be an extra?"

"It's a steady gig. I don't have dreams of making it big."

"I do," she said. "I always wanted to act. On stage, in movies. I have an audition for a commercial next week. After that, who knows?"

Before she could tell me more, a PA called all zombies to set. I glanced back as I walked away and saw that familiar puzzled look on her face. There was something about me that was different, but she hadn't figured it out yet. I didn't want to be there when she did.

The next day, I saw Shelly standing in a crowd of other villagers waiting on cue. Plenty of the other women on set looked like movie stars or acted like they did. But they definitely never gave zombies—or one-armed veterans—a second look. Shelly was normal-pretty; perfect for commercial work. And she had those eyes. Most importantly, when she saw me looking at her, she didn't run away screaming.

I hadn't wanted to get to know a girl, really know one, in a long time. I wanted to tell Shelly that I lost my arm being a hero, but the boring reality was that I was a cook. I was part of the Quartermaster Corps: peeling potatoes, checking inventory, driving supplies. That's what my team was doing when we drove over the IED.

Home from Afghanistan, I crawled into my parents' basement, living on daytime TV and beer, and listening to my parents argue about me. On Sundays, my high school buddy Bruce would come over to watch football or baseball. We rarely talked about anything other than sports but sometimes he couldn't help himself.

"Come work for me," he said one day. "A waiter quit last night. Could use another pair—"

"Don't say it."

"—of hands. You know what I mean."

"Don't you think I need two hands to carry food?"

"No."

"Then you're an idiot."

"What about Jim Abbott? People thought a major league pitcher needed two hands."

"That's different and you know it."

"You think waiting tables is harder than pitching?"

"Fuck you, Bruce."

"You can't stay down here forever."

"Why not? Free food, free healthcare, free TV. What else do I need?"

"Friends? Fresh air? A shower?"

I shook my head and pushed him out. The next Sunday, I wouldn't let him in until he promised not to talk about fresh air ever again. And back then, I certainly didn't want to make new friends.

At the VA center, the girls I met were either lonely, crazy, or both. For a while I hung out with a Navy vet named Gail, who was as miserable as I was. Her right leg was gone from the knee down. Those were dark months for us; sloppy sex after drinking ourselves stupid. Finally, she told me she was ready to lighten up and I was just keeping her down. I stole money from her purse and avoided her at the VA.

As part of rehab, I was supposed to attend group therapy three times a week, but it bummed me out too much. Everyone in the group was missing some part. One Marine in a wheelchair was basically just a torso and he was engaged to be married. Happiest motherfucker I ever met. I'd kill myself and this guy'd feel sorry for me. I hated myself but hated being with them even more. I spent the sessions at a coffee shop down the street, walking back to the VA before my mom pulled up to the curb.

Months later, during a ride home, I saw my misery reflected in my mom's face. Bruce was right. I had to do something to show her I was moving forward. The next day, scanning the VA job board, I saw a flyer for vets to be extras in a horror movie. Last thing I wanted to do was pal around with other freaks like me, but my options were zero and none.

I took that gig, and every other movie I could get, to give my mom a break from looking at my dumb face. But the other reason — the one that maybe I could tell Shelly — was that dressed as a zombie or a mummy or a monster, I was just another actor. On the set of horror films, the percentage of extras missing an arm or a leg was pretty high. Half the time, the normals didn't even notice anything was missing, if they noticed us at all.

On days I was called, I rode the bus to set early to get out of my mom's way. I got coffee and checked the call sheet to see if Shelly was on it. If she wasn't, I hung out in the makeup trailer with Rosie, the zombie specialist. If Shelly was called, I sat at a table by the forest and waited for her to find me. While I knew the odds for romance were against me, it was nice just talking with her.

"Hey, Number 22."

I looked up to see Shelly waving a paper bag at me. "I assume like all males — human or zombie — you enjoy chocolate donuts."

"If you must know, I was killed by diabetes, not Zed."

She laughed and set the bag on the table by my right side. While she never mentioned my lack of left arm, she obviously had noticed it. Maybe telling her over donuts would be less embarrassing for us both, so I told her what happened.

"I did notice more people with only one arm or leg than I've ever seen before."

"Told you it's a steady gig."

"Isn't there any other job you want? Extras don't make much."

"I do need another job. Want to pay my mom rent or even get my own place."

"Aren't companies always bragging about hiring vets? Can't be that hard, can it?"

"You'd be surprised," I said and changed the subject.

After the day's wrap, I took the bus to Bruce's restaurant. When I walked in, he just nodded. Once the place closed, I carried dishes from the kitchen to the tables and back but could only manage two at a time in one hand. At the end of the night, I swept up a heap of broken glass and plates.

"Don't worry about it," Bruce said. "Come back tomorrow."

After two weeks of practice, I could balance a tray of plates and glasses in my right hand, while tucking the tray stand under my left stump. There was just enough stump to grab an object, like you hold a pillow under your chin while putting on its case. That was how my stump and armpit worked. *Look Mom*, I wanted to tell her, *I didn't lose an arm, I gained a chin!*

On our last day of filming, Shelly and I waited together for the restart call. A light had blown and we had to wait for a replacement.

"How'd the interview go?" she asked. "Pasta place, right?"

"The manager was an asshole," I said. "When I held out my resume, he let it just fall to the table. *Nothing against the handicapped,* he told me."

"But if you could do the job, why wouldn't they hire you?" she asked.

"Come on, you can't be that naive."

Shelly looked away.

"I'm sorry," I said. "But why pick me versus a two-hander?"

"You could sue for discrimination."

I shook my head. The crew chief yelled for us to take our places.

"Don't give up," she said. "They're not all going to be jerks."

When the scene was done, I followed Shelly to the edge of Main Street, where the assistant director announced which villagers were going to die and which zombies would die again. Shelly took her death in stride.

"Maybe you'll come back as a zombie in *Stabby Stabby, Death Death Part 2*," I said. "*The Unstabbing*."

She laughed as the director called the doomed villagers for their final scene. "Bunch of us are heading to The Bitter End after wrap," she said. "You should come."

"Maybe." I hadn't been there since too many extras discovered it. As Shelly disappeared behind a burned-out building, I headed to the zombie trailer.

"I won't get in the way," I said when Rose saw me open the door.

She was working on Zed, who was filming pickups later. I took a tray of dirty brushes over to the sink and set them up to soak. I wiped off my makeup, trying not to stare at Zed in the mirror. He was one of those extras that would be in the majors soon—six two, broad shoulders, his jawline too rugged to be hidden by fake blood and scars for long. Through the thin walls, we heard the director call wrap.

"You going?" Zed asked, looking at me in the mirror.

"I'm not a happy-hour kind of guy."

"Come on," Zed said. "A couple of the extras are hot. I'm sure there's a Mrs. Zombie out there for you."

Zed was a dick but I couldn't let Shelly go that easily. I took the bus from the studio to the bar. The stop was about ten feet from the door so I could stand in the shelter and watch people come and go without being noticed. When the door opened, music and laughter floated out. I wanted to walk in, find Shelly, and tell her how I felt.

I used to be that guy. In high school, I was the left-handed ace on the mound, had a couple of girlfriends, and dreamed of pitching in the majors. My whole life ahead of me, my parents told me. But the scouts weren't impressed, so I chose the Army over community college. Then the IED went off, making me a right-hander with no prospects.

The door opened and Shelly came out with Zed. Of course he was there first. He'd never need to take a bus. I stepped out from the shelter.

"Hey, Shelly. Zed."

"Vic, you made it." She smiled broadly. Not acting, I thought.

"We're going to eat," Zed said. "You can come along if you want."

"No, but thanks," I said. "Just wanted to ask Shelly something."

"Sure," Shelly said.

"I'll get the car." Zed walked down the sidewalk like a man not threatened by anything, least of all me.

"You're not going in?" Shelly asked.

"It's not really my scene."

"What's your scene?"

I looked into those green eyes, still smudged with makeup that wouldn't come off without scrubbing. "I don't really know, if I'm being honest. But I was wondering. Do you think a dead villager like you would ever go out with a zombie like me?"

She smiled and not like a girl-turning-you-down kind of smile.

"If I'm being honest, I always had a thing for zombies. What do you have in mind?"

"I'm not sure," I said. "I just didn't want today to be the last day I ever saw you."

Shelly looked at me for a long second then asked for my phone. She typed in her number and handed it back. "Maybe I can help you figure out your scene."

That night, Bruce offered me a job.

"Thanks," I said. "But I can't make the kind of money I need here. Any other ideas?"

"Let me make a call." He held up his hand. "I know you don't want help, but fuck off."

Bruce got me an interview at a small restaurant in Silver Lake that did a lot of catering, where the real money was made. It would take nearly an hour, but I could walk there from my parents' house.

The manager, a brisk dark-haired woman, didn't mention my lack of an arm. "Let's see how you do," was all she said and handed me an apron.

Since it was past lunch, there were only a few customers left. I cleared the empty tables, making one more trip than a two-hander would but not dropping anything.

"Excuse me," a woman called out. "Would you make change for me?" She pressed a ten into my hand. When I returned, she took the change, ignoring me the whole time. I'd never been so happy to be invisible. The manager said she'd call in the morning.

That night, my mom dropped me half a mile from Shelly's place. I walked slowly so I wouldn't be too early. Or too eager. But I was both. I had a date with a woman with beautiful eyes and dreams of the future. At her door, I held my breath and knocked. Shit was about to get real.

All the Kids Are in Therapy

Life was just a series of soon-to-expire sticks of string cheese but my brother, a monster with no imagination, ate his by biting into it, like it was any ordinary food, whereas the rest of us—and, by us, I mean all of humanity—pulled the strings off one by one, dangling them, slurping them like spaghetti, whipping each other's cheeks with them, like normal kids and it makes you wonder what happens when a monster grows up and gets a job, and that's when the therapist asked if I had a happy childhood and I hesitated, wondering if she really wanted the truth or rather the abridged version I gave everyone else because, while people loved to hear a tragic story, they preferred it in the third-person and that's when I realized I was reclining on a couch, like a patient of Freud, and the couch wasn't for my comfort but for the therapist, so she didn't have to look me in the eye when I opened my heart and let the truth rush out.

Current Disasters

Lorrie sat on the couch in the cozy living room, drinking black coffee from a yellow mug and waiting for Grace. Art had told her not to wake Grace for any reason. Maybe if the house was on fire, he added, but call him first.

The week before, Lorrie overheard a counselor at the halfway house say his brother's wife needed a live-in helper to cook and clean. Lorrie didn't have anywhere to go once she was released, so she lied and told him she had experience as a house-keeper. Now here she was, her first day living with strangers in a cottage on the coast of Northern California. It wasn't even a town, really: just two neighborhoods of small homes connected by a tunnel under the coastal highway. Population 85. Now 86.

Grace had multiple sclerosis, and it had become worse in the past year. She was still mobile, especially with her wheeled walker, but couldn't stand for very long. She couldn't drive, and never liked to cook. The neighbors were helpful, Art told her, just not very interesting. Grace needed company during the day, while Art was at his studio in the city, 90 minutes away.

"Good morning!"

Lorrie turned to see a woman in the bedroom doorway, clutching the doorjamb. She wore a silk pajama suit.

"So, you're here to help?" Grace smiled. "Come on."

Lorrie made her way around the couch, trying not to stare, but didn't want to avoid looking either. Grace's legs bent awkwardly at the knees; but, other than that, she seemed perfectly fine. Beautiful, in fact, despite her short, dark hair mussed and a deep pillow crease on her cheek.

Lorrie helped Grace scoot onto the couch.

"Let's take a look at you," Grace said.

Lorrie didn't flinch under Grace's scrutiny. She'd been handcuffed to a hospital bed, sent to jail and rehab, and attended more NA meetings than she could count. A stranger examining her bleached-out hair, sloppy clothes, and bad teeth couldn't hurt her. If Grace deemed her unworthy to spend the day with, then that's what she deserved.

Grace smiled up at her. "You look like you can catch me when I fall. But can you cook?"

"Scrambled eggs."

"With cheese, please."

"Coming right up."

Lorrie's bedroom was behind the kitchen. The room was small, but she didn't have much—one suitcase of clothes, and a shoebox with her 90-day NA chip, an old photo of her mother and brother, two romance novels lifted from a bookstore, and a few other mementos.

The small bathroom across the hall was just for her use. After sharing a bathroom with three women for six months, a private shower with lavender-scented soap felt selfish.

The days quickly fell into a rhythm. Art was gone before Lorrie's alarm went off. The cottage was so small it took no time for Lorrie to straighten up, dust, do laundry and water the indoor and outdoor plants. By the time Grace woke up around ten, Lorrie had coffee and eggs ready, which they ate while reading the *New York Times* and the *Chronicle*. Grace read them both, front to back, while Lorrie looked at the lifestyle sections.

They went out for a late lunch every weekday, usually in Santa Rosa but sometimes down the coast. Everyone, everywhere, knew Grace, and she knew them all by name: busboys, owners, other customers. Lorrie was awed by Grace's calm, positive manner when she had every excuse to be bitter. One time, she tripped as Lorrie helped her out of the car, and they both went down hard. Lorrie sat stunned as Grace just laughed.

"You all right?" Lorrie asked.

Grace felt her legs and arms.

"No broken bones, no bleeding. Different day, different disaster," she said.

Art was usually home by seven and helped Lorrie finish dinner. She started with simple foods she cooked for her brother after their mother died: mac and cheese with broccoli, pot roast, stuffed bell peppers. Since Art was a food and lifestyle photographer, there was always a magazine with new recipes around. Two evenings a week, Lorrie drove to Safeway in Santa Rosa for groceries and the expensive wine Art liked.

The first time she stood in front of the wine display, her hands shook so much she didn't dare touch a bottle. She retreated with the cart to the cereal aisle and scribbled three things on the back of the shopping list: buy exactly what they ask for, put temptations out of sight, know you're not alone even when you're alone. Lorrie took a deep breath and smiled, thinking how annoyingly proud her sponsor would be. Back in the wine section, she put the bottle in her cart, and put a bag of spinach on top of it.

That night, she grew light-headed watching Art uncork a bottle. Maybe a drink—without a chaser of pills—would be okay. But she managed to decline the glass Art offered. After that, he filled the glasses in the kitchen, not bringing the bottle to the table. Lorrie was equally irritated and relieved.

Her strategy for Grace's medication was the same: keep it out of sight. Lorrie took the mailed prescriptions and any pharmacy bags Art brought home to their bedroom and set them on the dresser. None of it was her business, she thought as she closed the door.

In the evening, if it wasn't too cold, the three of them traveled slowly along a well-worn path to the bluff to watch the sunset. Grace used her walker, refusing to let Art carry her.

"I want to walk for as long as I can," she told Lorrie.

When they reached the bench that Art had installed, Lorrie picked her way down the short cliff to the water, happy for some silence. She and Grace chatted all day long. The half-way house was full of noise and voices, even in the dead of night. But here, the waves became white noise, and Lorrie felt calm at the edge of the world.

The ocean reminded Lorrie of her mother, though they'd never gone to a beach together. Once her mother told her that standing on the beach felt like being born again, and Lorrie had never forgotten.

Her mother said that when she stood at the ocean, with her face to God, there was only the future, no past. This scared Lorrie as a child — the vastness of nothing ahead and behind — but, on the evenings when it was just her and the waves, she felt closer to understanding.

On the weekends, Art and Grace went for a long drive or to dinner and a movie. Lorrie borrowed Art's bike and rode along Highway 1. Sometimes, she stopped at the library to check out a romance or young adult book. She liked reading about girls and women whose biggest problems were secretly being a princess or picking between the bad boy and the boy next door.

Other days, she biked through the tunnel to the other neighborhood and stopped for a soda at 7-Eleven. There was a dive bar at the far end of the strip mall, but Lorrie forced herself not to look at it. She concentrated instead on the people walking in and out of the other shops, living, what she assumed, were uncomplicated lives.

One Saturday afternoon, Art and Grace left for the city. They had tickets to the symphony and would stay overnight at a hotel. Lorrie listened to music while she folded laundry and baked banana bread. She vacuumed and read a library book. After dinner, she had nothing left to do. It was still light outside, so she took off on the bike. She rode along the highway, telling herself she was just going where the road took her. Ten minutes later, she was in the parking lot of the strip mall.

The door to the bar was open, and she heard faint conversation and music. Drinking wasn't her biggest problem. One drink wouldn't ruin her situation.

As she argued with herself, a man with a wild red beard and a "Free Mustache Rides" T-shirt stepped out to smoke. He offered Lorrie a cigarette. She shook her head.

"You must be new." He blew the smoke over her head. "I would have remembered you. What you got to say on this fine day?"

Lorrie peered beyond him into the bar, imagining the dark walls and the smell of stale beer. All of it—including the face of the man leering at her—was as familiar as her worn jeans.

"You have a great day, sir." She turned and unlocked the bike, thinking only about getting home as fast as she could.

Going through the tunnel, she rode over a small pothole. She flew over the handlebars, sliding across the dirt and gravel. When she felt steady enough, she sat up and took inventory: ripped jeans, a bloody knee, nothing broken. Just the current disaster, as Grace would say.

Lorrie walked the bike the rest of the way. She let it fall to the driveway and went through the back door. Art was in the hallway, just a few steps away from her. Lorrie let out a startled scream, and he stepped next to her.

"Shhh, Grace just got to sleep. Wait, what happened? Where were you?"

"Out riding. I crashed. I thought...you aren't supposed to be here."

"Your head. Jesus, your leg."

He led her into her bathroom, and she sat on the closed toilet.

"Hit a pothole," she said.

"Be right back."

Lorrie examined her leg, picking bloody pebbles out of her knee.

"Here." Art set antiseptic, paper tape, and a roll of gauze on the countertop.

"Why are you home?"

"We were at the opera and got a call. My mom fell. I brought Grace home. But I'm leaving in a second for Sonoma." His voice was a low hum in Lorrie's brain. She could still see the man in front of the bar and the inevitability of the night if she stayed. "I'm sorry I can't help. I have to get to the hospital."

"I know." Lorrie nodded, feeling sick. "Can I just ask you?" She looked up into his face. He was such a decent person. Had a career. Loved his wife. Wasn't an addict. "Do you ever get bored with yourself?"

"Uh, what?" Art turned back from the doorway.

"Just…can I…do you ever get bored with like, who you are?"

"Yeah, I guess," he shrugged. "Maybe we all do. Sometimes." He half-smiled. "I'm happy to talk later, but you have to figure it out for yourself tonight. I'm not sure when I'll be back, so please keep an eye on Grace."

"Of course," Lorrie said as the door closed.

In the morning, Lorrie waited until ten o'clock to make breakfast, thinking Grace would wake up any minute. At eleven, Grace still wasn't awake, so Lorrie ate and cleaned up. By the time she showered and dried her hair, it was noon and Grace was still sleeping. Even if she was exhausted from the night before, that was a long time to sleep. Lorrie called Art.

"Well, it's unusual, but I'm not worried," he said, "except she won't be able to fall asleep tonight. You can wake her. Just make sure you have coffee ready."

"How's your mom?"

"Just a sprain. Thanks. I'll be back in a couple hours."

Lorrie made another pot of coffee. She poured a mug—one sweetener and a splash of cream—and set it out with a homemade cinnamon scone.

She rapped on the bedroom door.

"Grace. It's time to wake up," she called. The snoring

didn't waver, so she walked in and sat down on the edge of the bed. "Time to wake up. I made coffee."

Grace's face was pressed into the pillow, mouth open, deep in sleep. Two amber-colored pharmacy bottles sat on the nightstand. One was empty, its cap on the ground. Lorrie picked up the other one and shook some pills into her hand. Methadone. Lorrie stared at the pills, remembering the daily line outside the clinic. Remembering the relapses. The broken promises. The last time she spoke to her brother.

She returned the pills to the bottle and shook Grace's shoulder. "Come on, Grace, wake up. It's afternoon, sleepy-head."

Grace stopped snoring but didn't wake up. Lorrie tried to lift an eyelid, like she'd seen nurses do, but didn't know what that was supposed to show. Grace was alive but why wouldn't she wake up? Lorrie ran into the kitchen and called Art again.

"She's not waking up. What do I do?"

He sounded too calm, as if this wasn't a surprise.

"First, go to the refrigerator. There's a list of phone numbers. When you hang up with me, call the neighbor listed first. Then call the second number."

Lorrie plucked the laminated list from under the magnet. The first number was Rhonda, who lived two houses away. The second was MedEvac.

"I'm calling a helicopter?" she asked.

"Hospital is too far away. Now hang up and call Rhonda, okay? Lorrie, you have to tell me okay."

"Okay, Art."

Lorrie called Rhonda, then went into the bedroom as the line rang for MedEvac. She only had to give the name. They had everything else on file, the operator said. The paramedics from the fire station would be there in six minutes, the helicopter not long after. Lorrie hung up and sat down next to Grace.

"Please wake up, please wake up."

Lorrie listened for the front door. By the time she

counted to ten, Rhonda still hadn't come. She shook out a pill from the bottle and slipped it into her pants pocket.

Rhonda burst into the room, the paramedics close behind her. Lorrie moved toward the window. She wanted to leave the room—there were suddenly so many people—but couldn't squeeze by the bodies and equipment.

"What happened?" a dark-haired paramedic shouted.

"She wouldn't wake up."

"How many did she take?" the other one shouted, sweeping the bottles into a plastic bag. "Did you see her take them?"

"No. I don't know. I tried to wake her up. Her husband's driving back."

The dark-haired one climbed on top of Grace with a syringe in his hand.

"Grace. Hi, Grace. Can you hear me?" He moved Grace's head back and forth. "Grace, you need to wake up, or I have to stick you with this."

Lorrie couldn't look away as Rhonda came to stand beside her.

"Sorry about this." He ripped open Grace's pajama top with one hand. "Here we go." In a fluid motion, the paramedic injected the needle into her chest, pressed the plunger, and withdrew it. He tossed the retracted syringe to the other paramedic and placed his hands on Grace's shoulders, as if bracing for a bomb to go off.

"What's happening?" Lorrie whispered to Rhonda.

"Maybe she took too many pain pills."

"Has she done that before?"

"I don't think so."

Grace's eyes opened, and she began thrashing against the paramedic's hands.

"Let me go," she yelled. "Son of a bitch, let go!"

Lorrie moved to the foot of the bed. "You're fine, Grace. Art's on his way. It's going to be fine."

Grace, panting, fixed her eyes on Lorrie, but didn't say anything else.

"I'm here," Lorrie said. "You'll be okay."

The paramedic motioned to the dark-haired one. "Get the board!" He had to shout as the sounds of the helicopter flooded the room.

Grace was no longer thrashing as they moved her onto the board. But her breathing was ragged, and tears fell from the corners of her eyes. Lorrie had to look away.

As Rhonda followed the paramedics out the front door, Lorrie went into the kitchen. She laid the phone on the counter and hung the list back on the fridge. She stood in the kitchen, shaking, until the sounds of shouting, sirens, and the helicopter faded away. Everything was quiet again. She went into the garage and got the bike.

As she pedaled, she no longer saw Grace. It was her mother thrashing against the paramedics in front of Lorrie, who was 13 and unable to do anything but watch. There was no helicopter. No dramatic revival. No husband who would do anything for her. She just died and Lorrie could never change that.

She arrived at the strip mall and dropped the bike on the sidewalk in front of the bar. Inside, she sat on a stool, ordered a beer, and set the pill on the counter in front of her. She should get on the bike and go back to the house. Clean up Grace's bedroom and change the bedding. Ask Art how she could help. She thought of her scribbles on the back of the shopping list. You're not alone even when you're alone. It was so simple. All she had to do was climb on the bike and go.

Not the Worst Day of Your Life but Definitely Not the Best

When you wake up on the red-eye, the plane is just touching down. But not in Chicago. "No," the woman next to you says, angling her way into the aisle as if those three inches will get her anywhere faster. You look out the window, confused. You could be anywhere. "Chicago's frozen," she says. "This is Indianapolis."

You don't believe her until you're schlepping your luggage up an escalator, under a mural welcoming you to the Crossroads of America. You follow the others down the carpeted hallway. You don't realize you're now in a convention center until you see union staff rolling boxes and chairs through open double doors.

As you walk by, you see booths and tables inside the cavernous hall, and at every one of them is a casket or two. You nod in solidarity, feeling dead yourself. At some point, the convention hallway becomes the hallway of the hotel where they're putting you up for the night. You're past exhaustion but once showered and in bed, you can't sleep.

You go to the lobby, but the free coffee isn't out yet. A lanyard with a convention badge is hanging off a table near the cold fireplace. No one is there, so you slip it around your neck and find your way back to the convention center. At the empty registration booth, you grab a beige tote bag filled with brochures and magnets and, while your badge doesn't indicate early bird, the security guard waves you in without looking up from her phone.

There are hardly any people in the hall, just a few booth workers straightening tablecloths and filling bowls with hard candy. After a few aisles, you pause at a booth displaying two open, child-size caskets set up on a table. One has pink lining, the other powder blue. The inverse of newborn bassinets. You don't remember the color of your sister's casket, only the feeling of your dad's strong hand and the sound of your mother crying.

You move to the next aisle and stop at a booth called Family Values at Rest. The casket closest to you looks to be made of particleboard. You run your hand along the fake wood and cheap ivory satin.

"That can't be comfortable," you mutter.

"Never had a complaint." A man drinking a Dr. Pepper comes up beside you. He is wearing a seersucker suit with suspenders and a straw boat hat. Not something usually seen during a Midwest winter.

"How can someone rest in peace in something so flimsy?" you ask.

"You'd be surprised." He gestures to another casket, identical to the one up front but with black satin lining. The table has a step stool next to it. "Be my guest," he says.

"Why not," you say and set the tote bag inside where your feet will go.

The man helps you climb over the edge of the casket. You aren't claustrophobic. In fact, you've always loved the feeling of closeness. As a kid, you hid in the smallest nooks and cubbies you could find. Wrapped yourself up in blankets like a mummy at night. So when the man offers to close the top, you agree.

He was right, you think as the lid comes down. It's not uncomfortable. You're average-sized and, arms crossed over chest, your elbows just brush the sides. It's dark. The darkest, most comforting dark you've ever been in.

Suddenly you feel something on your left pant leg. You shake the leg but whatever it is only rests with more pressure. You raise your right foot to scrape it over the left but, in doing so, you raise the lid.

"Ready to come out?" The man's voice is muffled.

"No, I just—" Whatever was on your left leg is now on both. You imagine a snake, a hand, the Grim Reaper himself, and reflexively kick both legs, which punches out the bottom of the casket. The man yells. Light comes in but you can't see what's on your leg so you push out with your arms, and you are free.

You and the casket—now just pieces of wood with satin stapled to them—are at the man's feet. He is yelling and gesturing and red in the face and you don't wait to hear how much a broken casket costs. You see the tote bag on the ground. Not the Grim Reaper, just burlap straps that fell onto your leg.

You scoop up the bag and run down the aisle toward the doors. You flee into the carpeted hallway. The commotion behind you doesn't slow you down. The hotel lobby—maybe the coffee is ready—is just in sight as you're tackled from behind. Hitting the ground knocks your breath out and you feel ribs crunching. The tackler pins you down and is talking very fast.

You wonder if there is a convention hall jail, identical to the windowless airport and mall jails you've been in. As you pass out from pain, you think how even those days weren't the worst days of your life.

The Milkbone Deposition

The room where they held the deposition was warm and dense, like the last cup of coffee in the pot. They brought in a box fan when my soon-to-be ex-wife complained about the heat, but it didn't help. And the clicking of the blades just made me drowsy. I shifted in the hardback chair, willing myself to stop sweating.

I had just finished my shift, so I was still in my warm-weather postal uniform: white polo, blue shorts, white socks, black shoes. The last neighborhood on my route was close to the lawyer's office so I drove there without changing. Maureen wouldn't move the meeting time, hoping to make me late, another strike against me.

"Why don't we get started?" Russ, my lawyer, said. He'd worked for my dad a few times over the years. *I'm a business lawyer*, he said when I called him up. *Better a business lawyer I know than a divorce lawyer I don't*, I told him.

As Russ and Maureen's lawyer said legal things to each other, I scratched at the stitches on my thigh. They were just scabbing over. From experience I knew this was when they itched the most.

I didn't need to listen to know what the lawyers were saying: Maureen wanted more than half of the savings we built up. She wouldn't tell me why she thought she deserved more than half. Maureen wouldn't talk to me at all anymore, except through her lawyer.

Heartbroken as I was, half seemed reasonable to me. I'd give it all to her if she just told me why she wanted, or needed, so much. We didn't have any kids, not much debt. She could have the house; it belonged to her parents anyway. I had already moved into an apartment complex with a pool. I didn't swim but seeing the pool out my bedroom window made me feel like things weren't all bad.

"I remember there were a lot more bags of dog food in

the pantry," I began. "But I didn't see Edgar Allan Pug eating any more than normal. We didn't talk about getting another dog. And we didn't shop at Costco. Not that I knew of. So why so much—"

"Can you get to the point?" her lawyer interrupted. "It was a simple question. Why don't you agree to the terms?"

I ignored him. "I found a receipt on the table next to her purse—"

Maureen cut me off. "It was in my purse. Not on the table. He went through my purse."

"Before she ripped it out of my hand," I continued, "I saw Milkbone dog treats on the receipt. Two boxes. But I never saw any boxes and never saw Edgar eating a Milkbone. He's more of a raw antler kind of dog."

"I told you." Maureen kept her voice low, the one she used with her kindergarten class. "I was going to surprise you with another dog."

"When?"

I scratched at my thigh again and caught the hem of my shorts with my watch. The seam ripped and some bit of debris—like sand or breadcrumbs—fell to the floor. I smushed them with my shoe and pushed them under the table.

"I was looking for the right kind of dog," she said. "He was getting bit so much I didn't want him to hate dogs. I thought having two dogs would help. This is ridiculous. Just agree to the terms."

"Control your client," Russ said. He turned to me. "Go on."

"The way it works is like this." I stood up and walked over to the window. This was the tallest building in town. We were only on the fifth floor, but it was enough to see across the small downtown and out past the freeway. I was only up this far about once a year when Maureen and I rode the Ferris wheel at the county fair. I was surprised to see how much the town had spread out, like I was asleep the whole time it was happening.

"At first," I said, "each bite is judged individually. They look at the cost, the medical bill, what the insurance paid. Then, how much time off did I have to take, how long was I on desk duty. That kind of thing."

"The first bite wasn't much of a surprise," I continued. "And it didn't hurt too much. Stupid little Jack Russell named Sir Yaps-a-Lot. The payout—settlement—was eight thousand dollars. I wanted to put it into savings. We needed a new car, but Maureen wanted to replace all the appliances. It would make the house more valuable, she said, down the road. A few months later, another bite, right on the calf, by a hound mix called Jabba the Mutt. That was fifteen thousand. I was on crutches for about six weeks to get back from that one. She wanted a closed-in back porch so we could drink coffee outside even when it rained."

I turned from the window. Maureen's face was red; her lawyer had a tight grip on her forearm.

"Can we have a break?" her lawyer asked.

"We're just getting started," Russ said.

I sat back down at the table and sipped from the paper cup. The water was warm. "Anyway, the latest bite was by a cairn terrier—you know, like Toto. He was named Bilbo Flea-baggins." I clenched my fist, determined to stop scratching. "That one paid another fifteen thousand. We went to Hawaii for a week. First-class flights. New luggage. All-inclusive resort. I kept wanting to put some into savings but it's hard to argue with Maureen."

"Yeah, right," she snorted. "You never saved a penny before you met me."

It was true. Before we got married, I didn't have anything to save for.

"They told me that was it, though." I cleared my throat. "I got a letter saying that the payout for all future bites was just a thousand bucks each. A few days after that, Maureen said she wanted a divorce. I don't know why, we just had a great time together in Hawaii."

"Did she give you a reason?" Russ asked.

"She said in California you don't need a reason."

"True," her lawyer said.

"We just weren't right together," Maureen said. "I told you. It has nothing to do with the money."

I continued talking, not hearing her anymore. "Three big payouts was generous, they told me, anything after that was either bad luck or you were gaming the system. But how could you game a system of dog bites? Ridiculous. But then again, no one else in our county had ever been bitten more than twice. I looked it up."

"Can he just stick to the facts?" her lawyer interrupted.

I bent down and ripped open the seam of my shorts completely. I let the crumbs fall into my hand. It definitely wasn't sand. I picked out a larger piece, about the size of a pencil eraser, and put it on my tongue. It tasted like what I imagined a dog treat would taste like: dry with a hint of chicken.

Maureen watched me with disgust. "He's nuts," she said. "I think we can agree on that."

"I can't believe it." I wiped off my hands and sat back in the chair. "I joked once that she washed my uniform in steak sauce to attract the dogs, but she was actually sewing treat crumbs into my shorts."

"That is the biggest bunch of baloney I've ever heard," she said. "Even for you."

"After we moved into the house, she bought a sewing machine. Said she was going to make new curtains. I heard the machine going a few times but never saw anything new."

"Like you would notice new curtains." She had tears in her eyes. Real tears, I could tell.

"But we had fun in Hawaii," I said. "Remember the cocktails served in coconut shells?"

Maureen looked at me straight on. A shadow lifted off her face and for a moment I saw her remember how we learned to hula at a pig roast. Then she stood up. "That's over," she said.

She picked up her purse and walked out of the room.

The lawyers looked at each other, then at me. Maybe it was the heat, but I didn't have any fight left.

"Give her whatever she wants," I said.

I walked over to the fan and turned it off. From the window, I could see Maureen walking in the parking lot. I watched her car turn onto Route 4 and be swallowed by rush hour. I'd probably never talk to her again. I didn't wish her pain, but I hoped she was just a little heartbroken, too.

I'd delivered mail in our town for twenty years. I knew more than just who got a medical bill or a credit card offer. I knew how the Douglas twins were doing in college and when Mrs. Stone's mother died. And I kept their secrets, too, like when Marty on Wagner Road fooled the city into planting two trees on his property instead of one.

But there had to be a middle distance. Somewhere between watching life from the top of a Ferris wheel and being inside other people's lives. Gun to my head, I couldn't tell you what color the curtains were in our house or if there were curtains at all.

We Always Break Up Near Water

I.   We sit on the banks of the river on the last day of summer. The drought has left only a trickle down the center of the dry river bed, so there is no sound of water to distract us from the words hanging between us. Nothing will be final until one of us walks away.

II.   We arrive at a pool party hosted by your coworker. After starving myself to fit into a bikini, I need only three watery cocktails to trip and fall into the pool. You leave, embarrassed, and your boss has to drive me home.

III.   We stand near the confluence of two rivers in the middle of the country as we roadtrip from one coast to the other. Silence for miles, followed by sharp words stabbing each other until we're hollowed out. The next day we're overly polite, as if we just met.

IV.   We keep returning to each other, a bit out of love, but mostly out of fear. We're more miserable apart than we are together, we tell ourselves, holding space until someone better comes along.

V.   We end for good standing next to the ocean. Giving up like a bloody boxer who can't take another round. The tears you try to hide taste like the sea as I kiss you goodbye.

The Jumping-Off Point

His cannabis delivery was late. Again. When the knock finally came, Tyler opened the apartment door to find Virginia holding a bag of take-out Thai food.

"How you feeling?" She gave him a deep kiss on the lips.

"Better now." Tyler pressed her against the door, squashing the bag of food. "I can take a later flight," he whispered.

Virginia nudged him toward the couch. He opened a box of noodles, sniffed, then set it on the scuffed coffee table.

"No appetite?" she asked.

"You can have mine." Tyler texted another question mark. This dispensary was always late, but it was the only place that carried his favorite strain in edible form.

Virginia lifted a potsticker with chopsticks. "I could come with you. Meet your mom."

"There's better ways to spend a weekend than in Arizona in the summer. It's hot. Like hell's asshole hot."

"You don't want me to go?" She put her hand on his knee and moved closer.

They'd only been dating a couple months. Too early for parental interaction but time had suddenly accelerated. The news—cancer, aggressive—had steered their relationship onto the fast track.

"It's just, would you want to meet her if I hadn't...if I wasn't..." Tyler sighed. "Maybe next time, okay?"

There was a knock on the door. Tyler made the quick exchange, feeling better already.

He chewed an edible during the ride to the airport. The rest were packed into a one-a-day gummy vitamin bottle. His medical marijuana card was in his wallet. While cannabis was now legal in California, the laws in Arizona were murkier, so it was just easier to be prepared.

By the time he took his seat on the plane, Tyler was relaxed but alert enough to watch the safety demonstration. Dying in a plane crash, rather than of cancer, seemed like a joke God would play. To Tyler, the idea of death was like moving to Nebraska. He wouldn't see his mom or friends anymore. He wouldn't be in San Francisco—or anywhere—anymore. That idea he could handle. It was the slow-motion images he had to push out of his mind. His body in a coffin. His clothes hanging on a rack at Goodwill. His mom, alone.

Tyler rubbed his sunken stomach, finally sensing a rumble of hunger. He was down twenty pounds since he was last home. His hair would fall out when chemo started, the doctor told him. Tyler would shave it before it got that far. Maybe Virginia would shave off her long golden hair, too.

The blast of the late afternoon heat hit him like a backhand. People moved slowly, fanning themselves with hats and newspapers, anything to move the air.

"Hell would be a vacation from this," Tyler said to no one in particular as he stood in the rideshare line. He'd talked his mom out of meeting him at the airport, hoping their reunion would be less intense on her own turf. That idea evaporated when she opened the front door.

"You're so skinny," she gasped. "Oh my God, Ty. You didn't tell me…"

Any other day, he would tease her for being so dramatic, but he just hugged her, letting her tears stain his damp T-shirt. Finally he ushered her into the house, the air conditioning giving him instant gooseflesh. She quieted down but the panic in her eyes remained.

"It's all that tofu you eat," his mom scolded later as she set out the taco bar trimmings: black beans for him, ground beef for her.

"Tofu didn't give me cancer, Mom." For years he did everything right: avoided sugar and red meat, didn't smoke and ran three miles every other day. He didn't have to open the fridge to know his mom had cooked far more than the two of them could eat in a weekend. Pot roast with mushroom gravy. Lasagna. Cold pasta salad. Linzer jam cookies and German chocolate cake. Forget cancer. He'd have a heart attack by tomorrow.

After dinner, Tyler took a cold shower. As he toweled off, his calf began to spasm. "Ow, ow, ow."

"What's wrong?" His mom pushed open the door.

"Mom! Jeez." Tyler clutched the towel around his waist. "It's just a charley horse."

He sat on the tub edge and massaged his leg.

"Are you sure? Did the doctor tell you that would happen?"

"It's just a cramp. Anyone can get them, you know."

The look on her face stopped him.

"Mom, I'm sorry." He stood up and kissed her cheek. "Everything's going to be okay. It's just...Do you mind if I get out of here for a little while? I'll see if Motor's around."

She nodded and they both pretended she wasn't about to cry.

By the time Tyler walked from the house to Motor's truck, any relief from the shower had evaporated.

"You look like shit," Motor said, as Tyler closed the rattling door.

"Well, you know. Cancer."

"Nah. You're pale as fuck. What, you inside jerking off all day?"

"You still driving this piece of shit?" Tyler pulled a beer from the small cooler at his feet. Along the highway, subdivisions gave way to strip malls then arid open space. "Nothing's changed here."

"Isn't that why you left?"

"Don't start." Tyler gulped the icy beer, though the smell turned his stomach.

"Fixed your mom's garage door the other day. Made me take home a whole goddamn icebox cake. How'd she take seeing your skinny ass?"

"About as well as you think. How's your sister?"

This got a glance from Motor. "When I told her the news, she said she forgave you."

"So cancer—that's all it took?"

"Fuck off."

Motor pulled onto a dirt road and drove the familiar route up to the Gorge. After parking, Tyler carried the cooler while Motor lifted a set of golf clubs from the truck bed. They walked up the well-worn path among the shrubs and cacti toward the clearing. In the distance, voices of climbers carried through the hot evening air. Halfway there, Tyler had to set down the cooler and wipe the sweat from his face. He didn't exactly miss the desert, but the oppressive heat and kicked-up dust felt like home.

Tyler was eight the first time he camped with Motor and his cousins at the Gorge. At some unspoken signal during lunch on the first day, the older boys jumped up and dragged Tyler and Motor to the jumping-off point and tossed them over. Before he could scream, Tyler was in the water. When they surfaced, Motor was laughing but Tyler got out and ran into the brush to hide. He refused to go camping again until high school.

When they reached the clearing, Motor put down the golf bag and knocked a tee into the dirt. Tyler kicked a few rocks off the cliff. Across the expanse of water, a few boats were nosing back to the dock.

"Looked a lot farther when we were kids."

"You were such a chicken-shit." Motor put a ball on the tee. "Fore."

"Still am." Tyler stepped back as the ball flew by.

"So. How are you?"

"Other than the vomiting and insomnia?" Tyler selected a club and placed a ball. "Could be six months, could be six years. They just don't know. Mine's an unusual case, the doctor said. He also said I was exceptionally healthy."

"Except for the whole cancer thing."

Tyler swung as hard as he could, enjoying the smack of the club against the ball. "Except for that."

"You're killing your mom, you know."

"Is that right? You fix one garage door and you're an expert on my mom?"

"I see her a lot more than you do."

Throwing the club down, Tyler stomped into the scrub brush to take a leak. When he came back, Motor opened a fresh beer and handed it to Tyler.

"Don't be so pissy," Motor said. "Get over yourself and move back. What's so goddamn special about California anyway?"

Tyler picked at the beer label. He thought about Virginia. The coding job he could do from anywhere. The rent he could barely afford. "Not just my mom…" He turned to look at the pink sunset over the faraway canyons. Tyler had been friends with Motor since second grade, but could count on one hand the times they talked about death or love or fear. After Motor's dad died, they hit balls silently at this exact spot every night for a week. "I need to…I need to live more. Longer," he said. "You know? I just don't want to be dead yet."

Motor clinked his bottle against Tyler's. "I don't want you to be dead yet either. And if you want to talk about that, I'll try. Be a lot easier if we were in the same state."

It was past one a.m. when Motor pulled up to Tyler's mom's house.

"Maybe I'll text Amy," Tyler said before getting out of

the truck. "Did she really forgive me?"

"Just don't be an asshole. And leave me out of it."

Opening the front door, Tyler was surprised to see the kitchen light on. He shivered in the air conditioning.

"Mom?"

"Out back."

"Be right there."

In the bathroom, Tyler splashed water on his face and grabbed the vitamin bottle. If anyone needed to mellow out, it was his mother. She was on the patio, stretched out in a lounge chair, an empty wine glass on the table. He pulled over the other lounger and sat sideways on it.

"Mom, I think you should have one of these." He took two gummies from the bottle. "It's edible pot. Don't shake your head. It'll help you relax."

She waved him away. "I already had some wine."

"Did that help?"

She paused, then held out her hand. "What'll it do to me?"

"You'll just feel calm. I'll have one, too."

They watched the stars in silence.

"Did you know that they move the holes on golf courses?" Tyler asked sometime later. "So players don't get bored." His mom didn't answer so he raised his head to see if she was asleep. She turned to look at him.

"You know what we haven't done in a long time, Ty?" Her voice sounded far away. "Miniature golf. Remember that place with the windmill?"

"They have this thing, called a divot plugger," Tyler said. "Or maybe it's a pivot digger. Anyway, this thing digs a new hole and they use that sod to plug up the old hole."

"We called it goofy golf when you were a kid."

"It's just absurd. They don't change the size of a tennis court or baseball field because people get bored. I'm all for change, but some things should stay the same."

"Is that why you never played with Motor? He won all those awards."

He turned on his side to see her better. "How do you feel?"

"Good. Maybe? I can feel my heartbeat. Is that normal?"

"Motor was always a natural at golf. I liked books better."

"You were always a bookworm," she said softly.

Tyler looked at his mom's face in the soft light from the kitchen. The furrows on her forehead were gone and her eyes were shining. He wondered if she'd worry more or less with him in the next room. She began to snore. If he got up to grab a blanket, she'd wake up, so Tyler just lay back and let the cool night air settle in around them.

American Gothic Getaway

She left town while he was at the dentist.

"Just leave," her friends said, patronizing her with their sympathy but not offering to take her in for more than a night. No one wanted the drama that trailed her like a shadow. The shadow of a two-hundred-pound man-child who raged at everything.

She had given up trying to remember the good times. They were gone — the girl who smiled easily; the boy who made her laugh.

After six months of planning and more stealth than she thought herself capable of, the day had come. She pretended to be asleep as he made his morning sounds, counting his footsteps until he was out the door.

She left the apartment with only her work bag, turning west instead of east at the corner. She was just another commuter until she stepped onto the train at Penn Station and rode away.

Crossing into New Jersey, she thought about him sitting in the dentist chair, head back, vulnerable. She left a voicemail saying she'd be working late. Eat without her, she urged, knowing he'd come by the office to see if she was lying. For once, she was.

Twenty-four hours later she was in Iowa. He would be looking for her now; not frantic, just methodical. Tracing her search history, hacking into her email, rooting through the garbage. He would find nothing. She erased herself thoroughly from both their lives.

She stepped off the bus under a clear blue sky. The house stood by itself, even smaller than she imagined. The single gothic window on the second floor was the only interesting feature on the simple structure. Without it, the house would not have become a fixture of Americana.

She walked across the parking lot to the tiny visitor

center, crowded with calendars, puzzles, and postcards. The homestead caretaker, a Midwestern woman equal parts friendly and skeptical, took her cash deposit and six months' rent—laughably cheap compared to Manhattan. The woman gave her a county map and directions to the grocery store.

"No car?"

"No, ma'am."

"Use the bike in the shed. That'll do until the snow."

"Yes, ma'am."

"You won't complain now about the tourists. You signed the contract."

"They won't bother me and I won't bother them."

"I heard that before." The woman looked her up and down. On the phone, she told the woman she was an artist looking for a quiet place to paint. She must have passed muster because the woman finally shrugged and handed her the key.

"Follow me."

Inside the living room, the furnishings were just as sparse and early 20th century as she had imagined. Just five hundred square feet, the house would be cramped with anything but the basics. She'd never had so much space all to herself.

"It's perfect," she told the woman and began to climb the stairs.

The woman stayed downstairs, the enigmatic smile-frown never leaving her face. "You won't be too lonely now?" the woman called up.

She stepped to the gothic window. Beyond her new home there was nothing but farmland and trees. *Lonely* she had known for years. *Alone* was what she craved.

"No, ma'am," she said. "This suits me just fine."

Family Vacation Dictionary

Bagism The mistaken belief, as you check in six pieces of luggage at the airport, that you remembered everything you'll need.

Shamemist The middle-class guilt you feel during the taxi ride through poor neighborhoods that evaporates as soon as you step inside the resort.

Verandont The balcony you insist on having when you book the resort but don't use once during the vacation.

Alcothesia When you forget—mid-argument—why you're fighting with your spouse and concede the point so you can enjoy the free cocktail hour.

Serensalti The first taste of a perfectly balanced mouthful of flavor. *Example*: The sweet, sour, and salty euphoria of a sublime margarita on the rocks.

Glowful The aura of contentment when something enjoyable is finished, such as an intense sexual encounter or an amazing meal prepared and cleaned up by professionals.

Vistadread When you're halfway through an enjoyable activity and it feels like the end is only moments away. *Examples*: vacation, an intense sexual encounter, a pitcher of serensalti margaritas.

Alarm-sigh The panic followed by relief you feel when you wake up on vacation thinking you're late for work but can roll over and go back to sleep.

Ringlong   The memory of wanting to be married. *[Antonym]* Alonetion: The memory of reading a book uninterrupted.

Momflog   The regret you instantly feel after yelling at your kids in public.

Slowm   A leisurely yet focused swimming stroke that implies you always stay at hotels with swim-up bars.

Wist   The warmth you feel when you catch your children playing together sweetly and skip the dinner reservation because you don't want to interrupt the moment.

Lovestrong   The security you feel when you smile at your spouse over the heads of your children and know that, despite rough times, you can always count on each other.

Grittle   The grains of sand that continue to appear in your home and clothes for weeks after vacation ends.

Pangst   The comfort of being back home mixed with the desire to travel again.

Youthache   The hope that your kids are old enough to remember this trip. *[Secondary use]* The fear that you wasted all that money on a trip your kids won't remember.

The Uncluded

The only reason Nora insisted I come to dinner was that she needed another man. Her cousin cancelled at the last minute, leaving the ratio of men to women unbalanced and, to Nora, unacceptable.

"It'll be fine this time," she pleaded on the phone. "I promise."

I tried a few excuses, knowing they wouldn't take. The idea of spending another holiday alone was more depressing than spending it with strangers.

As I walked up the icy steps of the metro stop near her home, I relaxed my face into something near a smile. Frowning was my default. Nora deserved better, but was my friend anyway.

Nora Amarez—prom queen, Junior League president, high-profile attorney, mother of two adorable kids—couldn't be more different from me but was also the only one who understood me. Not that there was even the slightest chance it could be me. We'd been friends, just friends, since college.

I wished there was a universe in which the impeccable brownstone before me was my house. A universe where Nora was my wife—not married to prom king Gerry—and I was her normal, well-adjusted, non-frowning husband. But even in the possibility of infinite universes, that particular universe didn't exist.

It was a normal awkward dinner party. The crowd was a mix of Nora's family and orphaned friends like me. More than one person remarked how special it was to be in the nation's capital on Thanksgiving.

"That," I whispered to Nora as I helped her carry in platters of food, "is because they don't live here year-round."

It was the same with Memorial Day and Fourth of

July when tourists in their shorts and sandals with socks took over the District. Then they returned to the Midwest or New England, and D.C.—the company town—humped along again, doing the nation's business.

"Anyone watch that show on A&E about hoarders?" someone at the end of the table said during the lull between dinner and pie. "The last episode was a doozy."

My back stiffened and Nora glanced down the table at me. I kept my gaze on the flames of the centerpiece candles.

"A&E? I thought it was TLC," someone else said.

"Disgusting," Nora's husband, Gerry, said. "How can you watch that?"

"It's sad but fascinating," Nora's cousin, a blonde woman sitting across from me, said. "How can you not watch?"

"As a psychologist," another woman said, to a chorus of groans, "I find it interesting that the reason is always either raised in poverty by a Depression-era parent or compensation for lack of parental love during childhood."

I excused myself to fetch another beer. As I left the room, I heard Nora calling for a happier topic. Closing the refrigerator door, I was startled by a woman standing by the counter.

"Wow, you're quiet," I blurted out.

She smiled. "Is that for me?"

I handed her the beer and grabbed another one. The woman was short and overwhelmed by a dark mass of hair falling around her shoulders. Her light blue eyes were huge under a heavy fringe of bangs, like headlights emerging from a tunnel.

"You're Nora's friend from college, right?" she asked. "I'm Lily."

I nodded. "You look familiar."

"New Year's Eve. You left before midnight, which was odd, so I asked Nora about you."

"I had no one to kiss," I said without thinking. I tried to recall her from the party but all I could remember was my bitterness in the middle of all the celebration.

She smiled and asked if I wanted to go outside.

"It's freezing out there," I said.

She shrugged.

On the tiny balcony overlooking the alleyway, Lily shivered but shook her head when I offered to get her jacket.

"I'm just waiting for the idiot talk to pass," she said.

"Not a 'Hoarders' fan?"

"Nope." She looked at me. "You aren't either?"

"To be honest," I said, then stopped. Her face was so open, actually interested in what I was saying. But how could I be sure she wasn't like everyone else?

To everyone else, it's a joke. You wanted to describe a madman or lunatic, you just said "tinfoil hat" and everyone laughed. Even Nora.

I laughed, too, careful to match their mirth.

But I lived in that house. The one kids avoided on Halloween. The one with the Oldsmobile on woodblocks and aluminum foil on the inside of every window. My dad was the one in the tinfoil hat. Actually, he had three.

I didn't do much living there really. Slept in my room. Showered and ate some meals. I found ways to spend nearly all day somewhere else.

Early on, school became my salvation. Sports, clubs, extra study hall—anything that kept me away from home. There was also the mall and Tommy's house. He was the only one who didn't tease me about my home and, in return, I kept his family's secret. Unlike mine, his house looked normal from the outside. It was inside that was unlivable.

Those TV shows—Hoarders, Buried Alive—could be amusing, until you see it in person. Or live it. I don't know how Tommy survived. Maybe he didn't. We lost touch after high school.

His parents had a pathological problem that made them

unable to deal with the everyday flotsam of ordinary life. Each room was filled with towering piles of junk, on the floor, on the furniture, on every available surface. Newspapers, computer parts, gift wrap, plastic hangers, you name it, with aisles carved out so you could move through the house. Except for Tommy's room, which he kept locked at all times.

When his parents weren't looking, Tommy shoved trash into my backpack—empty tuna fish cans, broken Christmas ornaments—to throw out on my way home. Tommy and I thought his parents were just weird and messy. My dad, Tommy agreed, was certified crazy.

When I was growing up in San Francisco, my dad took me a few times to the Musée Mécanique at the edge of Ocean Beach. This was when he still went out into public, before the fear or insanity—whatever it was—set in completely.

The museum was tucked into a dark labyrinth underneath the Cliff House, next to the ruins of the Sutro Baths. The cave-like space, dusty and ancient, was full of carnival games and mechanical slot machines from forty years earlier. My father loved it.

Entering the museum, we were greeted by Laffing Sal, a behemoth of a woman, made of wood. She was painted so long ago that by the time I saw her she was just a grimy brown body with faded orange lips and hair. For a kid with a weird dad, not much creeped me out but I was nervous in that place, afraid to venture off by myself.

Many of the people I saw in the museum were like my dad, moving silently from dusty game to broken machine, touching them despite the admonishing signs. The most fascinating and repulsive game was the Opium Den, where tiny, vaguely Asian wooden figures reclined next to miniature pipes. I watched as my dad put in quarter after quarter, making the diorama come alive. He turned the knobs, making tiny puffs of smoke rise from the lips of the figurines. They would sit up, stretching their hands forward, grasping at nothing, before jerking back down on their tiny cots, waiting for the next quarter, the next hit to come. My dad would stay for hours if I didn't drag him away. As a kid, I didn't understand the look on my dad's face, his desperation as he slid in a quarter. Nostalgia for something—an era, a life—he could never have.

When I was twelve, my mom told me that my dad's family once owned a dunking-booth business, renting them out to festivals, church bazaars, and summer fairs.

"Dad was a carny?" I asked. That could explain my house, my family. "I'm part carny?"

"I guess so." She tried to smile but her lips just pressed tighter until they turned white.

I wanted that to explain everything. Grandma was the bearded lady. Grandpa swallowed swords. I tried so hard to believe there was a reason for it all.

Mom left Dad when I went away to college. She didn't divorce him. She loved him, she said, she just couldn't live with him anymore. She kept an eye on him over the years, paying his bills and bringing him groceries every week.

I told this all to Lily out on the cold balcony. I just kept talking, her wide blue eyes curious but not pitying. When I paused, she took a sip of beer and waited. She was actually listening, I realized, not just waiting for her turn to speak. I wanted to hear her story—and why she was so interested in mine—but couldn't stop talking.

Inside the kitchen, Nora and a few others were huddled over glasses of wine at the counter. Nora slipped off her cardigan and handed it to me along with more beer.

"Why don't you like Hoarders," I asked Lily outside as she pulled on Nora's sweater.

"Joanne? The blonde across from you?"

I nodded.

"Her parents were alcoholics. She is fucked up six ways to Sunday because of it. I wonder how amusing she'd find a reality show about growing up with an alcoholic. Finding your dad face down in his own vomit. Taking care of your younger brother because your mom's too bombed to cook."

"Sounds like a hoot," I said. "Real Winos of Georgetown?"

"The Secret Lives of Co-dependents?"

Our laughs turned into sighs.

"My parents were hoarders," Lily said after some silence. "Not criminally so. They'd never have their own TV show. Once a year we had a crazy clean-out-the-house week and a huge garage sale. No one ever wanted our junk so my dad and brother would spend another week hauling it all to the dump. We ate a meal or two in the dining room—we had this massive oak table—and then it would start all over."

"I never had friends over," she continued. "No sleepovers. Refused to let boyfriends in. I drove myself to my prom." She groaned. "I try to be grateful. I wasn't abused. There was food to eat. They aren't bad people. I tell myself they did the best they could, but still."

"I know," I said. "Turns out parents are just people, too. But by the time we figure that out, we're fucked in the head."

"Amen to that."

"To messy homes." I clinked my bottle against hers.

"To aluminum hats," she laughed. "Maybe they'll do a show about that, next."

"One can dream," I said.

A year later, Lily and I visited San Francisco. We decided to meet each other's parents and I thought visiting the Musée Mécanique would ease her in. We ate lunch at the Cliff House before I took her down to the beach. A sign on the locked door notified us that the museum relocated years earlier to a store-front on Fisherman's Wharf.

Lily took off her shoes and dug her toes in the sand. I stood at the edge of the water, tossing stones into the small, foamy waves. I thought of my father, who still lived in our house, still trapped by his own madness. I tried to picture him through Lily's eyes, wondering if he would seem as crazy to her as he did in my memory. Part of me worried that he wouldn't seem crazy enough. That I had imagined it all. Maybe I was the crazy one.

Lily took my hand and smiled. "If you're nervous," she said, "I'm right here."

Like all of Fisherman's Wharf, the Musée Mécanique was now safe and sanitized for tourists, not creepy at all. Inside, the machines were dusted and they gleamed in the sun streaming through the wall of windows.

But it was all there — the Opium Den, Naughty Marietta, and the Fortune Teller. When Lily wanted a closer look at Laffing Sal, with her repainted hair and lips, I held back. Spruced up, she was somehow even more unsettling.

At the house, the front steps were narrower than I remembered. Aluminum still lined every window; weeds grew high in the driveway cracks next to the rusted-out Olds. I squeezed Lily's hand as we reached the door, which was open just a crack. That was the only way I knew he was still inside.

Stuffed Peppers to Please Everybody

Ingredients:

» 8 peppers, hollowed out and blanched. Reserve tops.
» 2 pounds ground beef, browned like your skin on the last day of vacation, and drained.
» 4 cups white rice, cooked with extra water so it's really soft or your mother will complain.
» 2 big cans of tomato sauce. Not the generic brand; the cans that are red like the color of blood.
» Sugar, to taste. Your father in-law will say, "What is this, dessert?" but your parents won't eat it otherwise.
» 2 cloves garlic, diced.
» Onion, powdered or diced. Your mother-in-law doesn't like shortcuts, but you hate cutting onions; there's no feeling of relief from manufactured tears.
» Pepper tops, diced and sautéed with garlic and onion/powder.
» Spices, to taste: hot Hungarian paprika, smoked Hungarian paprika, sweet Hungarian paprika, salt, and pepper.
» 1½ cups cheese. Your mother likes mild Monterey Jack. Your father-in-law doesn't want any cheese, just a dollop of sour cream. Your dad and mother-in-law don't have a preference. Your husband doesn't know anything about cheese so you use what you like, sharp cheddar.

Directions:

Mix the stuffing ingredients, fill the cooked peppers, and top with cheese. Bake at 350 degrees for 45 minutes. Serve with three bottles of wine: a chilled sweet white wine for your mother, a Hungarian red called Egri Bikavér (Bull's Blood) for your father-in-law and husband, and a robust pinot noir for you and your dad. You'll drink most of the pinot yourself and flush as red as an unsweetened tomato when your parents begin suggesting names for grandchildren.

Chef's Notes:

1) After two years of dating, you traveled with your future husband to a small town outside Budapest to meet his extended family. You hoped he would propose during the trip, somewhere romantic, like on a bridge over the Danube that was the site of a historic battle. But for most of the trip, you sat by yourself reading a book while he spoke half English, half Hungarian to his relatives.

2) The first time you ate Hungarian food was also your first time experiencing heartburn. His great aunt's stuffed peppers weren't hot exactly. Just a slow burn that grew worse after you finished eating.

3) As the two of you walked a mile to a pharmacy for antacids, you spied a bridge in the distance. You asked your boyfriend if anything important happened there. He gestured at the bridge, the town, and the fields, and said there wasn't much of that land that hadn't been soaked in blood at one time or another.

The Poles of Inaccessibility

On the tarmac, four steps away from the plane, the intensity of the cold hit Lena. This wasn't just cold. This sensation was far worse.

Richie yelled for Lena to put on her goggles. The whiteness turned pink and Lena saw, about eight hundred meters away, what looked like a soccer ball half-buried in snow. As they turned from the plane, Richie shouted again but the wind carried the words away. Lena had no breath to talk anyway. She stopped moving. After a twenty-three-hour journey on four different planes from Kansas to the South Pole, Lena was too exhausted to move another step. About ten paces ahead, Richie turned around and headed back to her. He pulled his scarf down.

"In ten minutes, you can stop and sleep." He grabbed her sleeve and pulled her toward the soccer ball.

Lena woke up and rubbed her eyes, unsure if it was day or night. The only certainty was that she was alone in one of the seven most remote places on Earth.

When they reached the dome—six hours ago according to her watch—Richie grunted hello to Kevin, the researcher she was replacing, and pushed past him down the hallway. Kevin, who was leaving with Richie, gave Lena a quick tour of the dome: the meager research rooms and even sparser living quarters.

Lying in bed now, Lena hardly remembered any of it. Kevin had told her not to worry. All the protocols were written down along with tips from past researchers on how to survive her time.

Above her on the wall, rough scratches were etched into the fake wood paneling of the bedroom. Lena sat up and saw that the entire wall was covered with these shallow grooves.

She ran her fingers over the markings, wondering how long they'd been there. Lena groped through the nightstand drawer and found a chewed-up pencil. Starting a new row, she carved a fresh groove in the wall. One day down; 89 to go.

In the kitchen, Lena pulled on mittens and flicked on the heat source for the kettle. Even though the thermostat was set at sixty-six degrees, she couldn't shake the chill she had since stepping off the plane.

She rummaged through the cupboards to find coffee and powdered creamer. When the teapot whistled, Lena poured the just-boiling water into the French press and closed it. She stood there for two minutes and thirty-five seconds, hands on the counter with her fingers spread inside the mittens. She inhaled the smell of coffee.

Patrick's wife was the one who filed for divorce. At least that's what he told Lena. He wasn't wearing a wedding ring when they met.

At the start of the fall semester, Lena was walking by Anderson Hall when she was struck in the leg by a tennis ball. She looked up to see a man and a dog running toward her.

"Sorry about that!" the man shouted.

"It's fine," Lena said when he stopped beside her. She picked up the ball at her feet. The dog, a black and white Boston terrier, jumped on Lena to grab at the ball.

"Down, Diesel." The man, older than her by a few years, had shaggy blond hair and wireless glasses. He pulled Diesel by the collar. "He's mad for that ball. Throw it."

Lena hesitated, watching Diesel as Patrick let him go. The dog's eyes never left the ball in Lena's hand. She threw it as hard as she could across the field. Diesel gave chase like the ball was a squirrel covered in gravy, then mouthed the ball and streaked back to the man.

"I'm Patrick. Philosophy adjunct." He waved the red

plastic ball-thrower in his left hand. "This thing throws much farther than I can. Drop it," he said to the dog.

Diesel was pushing the ball into the open claw of the ball-thrower, reloading his own toy.

"If only he could throw it to himself," Lena said.

"Drop it." Diesel kept his mouth on the ball inside the claw and looked up. "I can't throw it unless you drop it," Patrick said.

"Why won't he let go?"

"He wants to chase the ball, but he also wants it already in his mouth." Patrick sighed. "Every single time." He twisted the claw away from Diesel and flung the ball across the field. "Probably the only dog at the shelter having an existential crisis and that's the one I pick."

After that, Lena made a point of walking by Anderson Hall whenever she was on campus. Diesel was fun and Patrick was interesting. But look where that got her. A semester of isolation, stirring evaporated milk into a cup of coffee, eight gazillion miles away from any other human.

Her instructions from Kevin indicated that there were enough tubes of permafrost in the walk-in freezer to get her through her three-month rotation at the "Shit-gloo," as he called it. He had gone outside enough to collect more samples than she would probably need. *But*, his notes said, *feel free to collect new samples, especially if you notice any changes in the temperature or angle of sunlight.*

She knew from reading Kevin's research and journal entries that he went outside far more often than any previous researcher. He even dove naked, once a week, into the snow-drifts outside the front door. *Best cleanser in the world*, he wrote.

He was insane, Lena assumed. Either was before or became so during his stint in the Shit-gloo.

After her initial trek from the airstrip, Lena never wanted

to go outside again. But by the end of the second week, the torture of watching the sun shine through the porthole windows of the dome was too much to bear. One morning, she pulled on her hat, scarf, and mittens, and poked her face out the door for as long as she could stand it, just to feel the sun on her cheeks. By the third week, that was no longer enough.

Twice a day, she methodically buttoned up her long johns, ski jumper, wool socks, plasma thermal jacket, mittens, scarf, fake-fur lined hat, and sunglasses.

If she worked slowly enough, she could stretch the whole process to thirty minutes: bundling up, opening the entrance, walking twenty paces, tilting her face toward the sun, then returning and unbundling.

Three meals, each drawn out to an hour, took up three hours a day. She slept for nine hours. Online entertainment and emails: two hours. Exercise: one hour. Reading: two hours. That left her six hours a day for her research on tracking the changes in the permafrost, which was not very interesting or challenging.

The water in the shower was room temperature at best, never hot, so Lena had spent an hour, every other day at first, heating up water for a bath, one teakettle at a time, like the pioneers. After a couple weeks, this became tiresome. She gave herself sponge baths. By the end of thirty days, she stopped bathing completely. Who was going to notice? Soon, though, her skin began to itch.

Her mother's biggest worry, mentioned in every email, was that the loneliness would become too much to bear.

"Are you sure you're fine? Not going crazy?"

She was "fine," she answered. Whatever that meant.

Lena was used to spending hours alone, many days at a time. Her interactions with her colleagues in the biology department, career researchers like her, were brief and awkward.

Only in Patrick had she found someone she could really talk to—she told him things she didn't discuss with anyone else. Her happy but unremarkable childhood. Her non-existent love life. Her dreams of being head of the National Institutes of Health. She hadn't permitted herself to imagine anything more, but it was nice to let someone inside her little world.

Loneliness, to Lena, was her Aunt Mary, who lived in an apartment near the center of their small town.

Aunt Mary had boyfriends over the years but never married. Sometimes Aunt Mary would bring someone to dinner but only a man named Stewart lasted more than a few months. He wore too much Old Spice but patiently taught Lena to play chess.

Before Stewart, Lena would sometimes spend the night at Aunt Mary's, the two of them tucked into parallel twin beds with matching floral comforters, eating popcorn and watching movies. But during the Year of Stewart, the normally separated beds were pushed together and covered with a blue and white striped bedspread. Lena never spent the night that year. She didn't mind, though. She liked thinking about Aunt Mary with Stewart, under one bedspread, like how her parents slept.

When the Year of Stewart was over, Lena assumed Aunt Mary would keep the beds pushed together and enjoy the extra room for herself. But when she invited Lena over, the beds were separated again, and the blue and white bedspread was gone. The beds were never pushed together again. That was loneliness.

The Shit-gloo was simply penance for happiness that Lena wasn't supposed to have.

As the days blurred together, Lena became more aggressive in her research, even though her faith that anything would change was fading. She doubted anyone would read her notes, but she wanted to signify her contribution. Record that she had taken up this particular space on the planet for this amount of time. If she didn't write it down, she came to believe, how could she even know where she'd been?

She knew climate change was real. She believed everything that had scientific evidence to back it up, but she wasn't worried that life as she knew it would end in her lifetime. And even if it did, would that be such a bad thing? Was it really her job—*homo sapiens'* job—to keep the world exactly as it was now?

By the end of the second month she began to wonder if maybe that would be for the best. The planet would rebel against the humans—no more oxygen in the air or a fatal lack of resistance to bacteria—and then it would peacefully begin again. They would become the extinct dinosaurs of a future civilization. This thought often comforted her as she fell asleep at night. If no one else existed, then she couldn't be alone.

Lena stood naked, shivering, just inside the closed entrance of the Shit-gloo. A hot cup of tea waited on the table. Towels and the down comforter were ready on the floor. The whole ordeal would take less than fifteen seconds.

She couldn't stand herself any longer. She smelled. She itched. She was ready.

On the count of three, she pulled open the door and dove, headfirst and screaming, into the six-foot snowdrift slouched against the dome. Before she closed her eyes, the whiteness of snow and the pain of the cold nearly blinded her. But Lena would survive. She had to.

Her Boyfriend with the Difficult Name

Every quarterback was named Steve.

Every cheerleader, Jennifer.

The captain of the baseball team? Michael.

She didn't see the overwhelming whiteness, the sameness, of her hometown until she opened her eyes in another country. She'd never even traveled to another state and here she was, three flights later, in a foreign land, as her mother would call it.

But she was the foreigner, unable to understand what the family was saying, her boyfriend translating every so often. Her boyfriend with the difficult name, her mother called him, refusing to learn how to pronounce it. As if he was named that just to cause trouble.

She imagined her mother arriving here for breakfast. Sniffing at the blood sausage, cheese spread, and bitter coffee the family offered. Unlike her mother, she dove into the food and the flow of words, grateful there was more to the world than what she'd always known.

The Other Side of Luck

"We should go up," Marco says, hovering behind me.

We've roamed the main casino floor for hours now, moving from slots to video poker to live games. At this hour, our blackjack table is the only action other than an old man talking to himself at a slot machine and a bored waitress approaching with another round of drinks.

"I'm keeping Jack company," I say, though I'm desperate for a shower.

"We have to be up in six hours."

"I'm still playing."

Marco pulls on his earlobe, his telltale sign of being annoyed, and sulks away.

"Life of the party, that one," Jack snorts. "Just like his mother."

It's not that I want to hang out with Jack, the 68-year-old groom-to-be and Marco's future stepfather, but I don't want to be in bed with Marco either. I should have broken up with him a month ago. I should have moved out of the apartment by now. And I definitely should not have come on this trip. But Angela, Marco's mother, asked me to be her only bridesmaid; I don't want to disappoint her. Plus, I've never been to Las Vegas and Angela is picking up the tab. If that makes me a whore, so be it.

All I know about Jack is that he loves baseball, doesn't respect Angela and, even at his age, is a mama's boy. His mother, Beatrice, is 90, deaf, and a pain in everyone's ass. Thankfully, she's too frail to make the trek from San Diego.

"Gentleman has twenty-one." The dealer pays out, then sweeps up our cards. Jack has won four in a row.

"You have all the luck," I say.

The waitress hands us the drinks.

"Bachelor's luck. We'll see what happens tomorrow." Jack drops two one-dollar chips onto the tray. "I'm getting hitched in the a.m.," he says to the waitress, who ignores him. Jack leers as she walks away and I want to punch him.

"Congratulations to the gentleman," the dealer says.

"Angela will be my third wife," Jack replies.

"Third?" This is news to me. "I thought she was your second."

"Actually, third wife, fourth marriage. One poor gal married me twice." He grins. "If this one doesn't work out, I'm going to start thinking it's me."

I stare at my cards as Jack laughs. I used to think about marrying Marco but not anymore. "And you're ready to do it again?"

Jack taps on the felt. "Love's like toilet paper. You don't know how important it is until it's not there." He waits but I don't laugh.

"You loved them all?"

"Close enough, I guess."

I look at Jack's thinning white hair and deep neck wrinkles. If I were Angela's age and scared to die alone, I'd settle for close enough, too.

Another drink and I stumble up to the room. I slide into bed fully clothed, reeking of sweat and Jack's woodsy cologne. I hold my breath as Marco stirs but doesn't wake.

The four of us wait outside the casino entrance for the wedding limo. Even in the shade, the sun feels brutal on my hungover eyes. At night, the Vegas Strip — dressed up like a showgirl — dazzled me but now, with its unlit neon and garbage streets, it's just another ugly desert town.

"Look," Jack says.

We turn to watch him pick up something from the sidewalk.

"A lucky penny." He flips and catches it in the air.

The ride is quiet. Jack rubs his penny. Angela fidgets with her skirt while Marco looks at his phone. I stare out the window, wishing for a sweater. My short lavender dress seemed perfect for the desert but now I feel overexposed. When I reach for Marco's hand, he pulls away. I don't really want to hold hands but a wedding is supposed to be romantic, and I'm annoyed that he's annoyed with me.

The Little Chapel of Flowers sits at the end of a generic strip mall. An overdressed lady ushers Angela and me into a small room while Marco and Jack meet with the minister. Angela refreshes her lipstick as I imagine Jack paying the fee with casino chips.

"How was your night?" Angela asks. "Blackjack?"

"Good, good." I look around the room. A vase of fresh flowers and red velvet chairs make it less cheesy than I thought it would be. "To be honest, I owe Jack forty dollars."

She laughs dryly, not at all the throaty, delighted sound she makes at Marco's jokes. "Don't worry about that. I won four hundred dollars on my way up to bed last night. First slot I pulled."

"I should have stayed with you."

"I'm glad you two had some time together," she says. "Feels like my family is coming together. It's just been me and Marco for so long, you know." She takes my hand and pats it.

I kneel by the chair, cold and awkward in my thin dress. Her sincerity embarrasses me. "I just thought Jack could use some company," I say.

"I'm sure he loved it. He hates to be alone. I always go to bed hours before him and he always complains. He thinks I should stay up. I think he should come to bed earlier."

"And you can't compromise?"

"He said he's too old to compromise."

"What? But—"

She smiles. "Can I ask you…Do you think…" Her voice breaks. She's still holding my hand and I feel hers shake. "Is this silly? A Vegas wedding? It sounded romantic, but now that we're here, maybe it's crass." She's squeezing my hand now. "You'd never have a wedding like this, would you?"

I glance at the closed door, wishing Marco would come in. "Oh, I don't know. I mean, I can imagine the dress and the cake. Chocolate, of course. But I can never quite see who the groom is."

"Not Marco?"

I look at our clasped hands. Her nails are painted deep pink, with a big turquoise ring on her right ring finger. I wonder what kind of wedding ring a cheapskate like Jack bought.

"I'm sorry," she says. "That was rude."

"It's just...this is why unmarried couples shouldn't go to weddings. It's too much pressure."

"No pressure, I swear." She smooths a piece of hair out of my face. "I just see how much Marco loves you, and I don't know if I love Jack like that. And...shouldn't I love him like that...if I'm going to marry him?" She lets go of me and fusses with her lipstick case. "What do you think? Marco won't tell me what he really thinks."

"Everyone gets cold feet."

She shakes her head. "It's not cold feet. You've seen Jack...sometimes he, well, he can be a jackass."

"All men are like that sometimes."

"Marco isn't, is he? I hope not."

Marco is a jackass sometimes, but no mother wants to hear that. And I've been a jackass for weeks. Too much of a coward to just tell him the truth and let him get on with his life.

"I just couldn't find a reason to say no," Angela says when I don't answer. "If only he hadn't asked."

No, I think. *No one should ever marry Jack again.* "I'm the last person you should be talking to about love," I say.

"Why would you say that?"

I want to tell her that I know less about love than anyone. For two years I was ridiculously in love with Marco, like I couldn't breathe when he wasn't around. Of course I pictured our wedding, and more. But then, brushing our teeth one Tuesday night, it was gone. Nothing had changed between us, but the love was gone. And that's what I couldn't understand.

I always thought that once you found love, you kept it forever, like a stone you picked up at the beach and put in your pocket. Even if you broke up, the love was still there. But maybe, sometimes, the stone slips from your pocket and you don't notice. It's just gone. And, like Jack, you start over.

Angela's eyes search mine; I have nothing to say.

There's a rap on the door and I hear Marco whisper, "It's showtime."

An hour later, we're on the highway back to the Strip. Our exit is the next one, I think, anxious for champagne. I'm next to Marco, facing the rear of the limo. Through the small back window behind Jack and Angela, I see traffic building. Our limo slows down. I keep my eyes on the window and see a blue truck coming up fast behind us.

"It's not stopping!" I shout.

No one hears me, they just kept talking about dinner. I shout again and grip the edge of the seat. I wonder vaguely if I'm wearing a seatbelt. When the truck slams into us, Angela and Marco are thrown to the floor at our feet. Jack and I manage to stay seated as metal scrapes and glass shatters. The limo lurches forward.

I turn to the front and look through the open privacy window. We're rolling toward a shallow ditch that drops off the side of the highway. The driver, a huge Samoan man stuffed into a faded tuxedo, is slumped over the steering wheel, groaning.

"We need to stop!" I reach through the window and smack the driver's shoulder. "The brakes! Hit the brakes."

He moans louder. I look back at the others—Jack is

yelling at Angela as Marco claws at the locked door. I start to climb through the privacy window, scraping my shoulders on the sides. My dress rips as I struggle. There is no way I can fit through.

The driver is now quiet but his eyelids flutter. I stretch across him to grab the wheel and yank it to the left, aiming us away from the ditch. Jack and Angela's fresh vows hang in the air, *'til death do us part.*

I slap the driver's face until he opens his eyes. He engages the parking brake and unlocks the doors. I ease myself back through the window. Angela is on the floor, crying and grabbing her neck. Jack shushes her like a child. Marco is outside yelling at a guy on a phone. I hold my dress together with my hands. It's not until we're in the ambulance that I notice my shoulders are bleeding.

We're in the emergency room, a thin curtain separating our beds. The truck sustained the most damage, though you wouldn't know it hearing Angela cry. Marco whispers to me that, other than a strained neck, she's fine. Just a panic attack. First from being strapped to a stretcher and then from being in the hospital. I want to say that maybe the reality of marrying Jack finally hit her.

"How do you feel?" Marco asks.

"My neck, shoulders hurt."

"Painkiller should kick in soon." He pauses. "I should go to my mom."

"Jack's with her. What about me?" I ask.

"You'll be fine without me." Marco looks me in the eyes for the first time in weeks. I try to smile but we both feel the truth hanging between us. He gives me a little wave and disappears through the curtain.

I wonder if they will send a replacement limo to take us to the hotel and if Angela will get in it. The odds of our limo being hit twice in one day are low, but I doubt Angela wants to hear any theories about luck and chance.

Whatever Marco is saying to Angela works. Soon we buckle our seatbelts in a new limo with a new driver. I can't look at Marco as he fusses over Angela.

"Just think how it could've turned out," Jack says, "if I hadn't picked up that penny."

Later that night, I break up with Marco, even though it means I'll sleep on the loveseat, which makes every pain from the day worse. Angela would probably pay for another room, but I can't bear to add any more disappointment to her wedding day.

Deadstock

Even with air conditioning, the warehouse was never cool. In the afternoon, the sun came through the windows on the west side, heating the seamstresses until they were tender and limp at the end of the day.

Thaya took two gulps from her water bottle, then selected a small swatch from the heap of material on her left. She chose a scrap of dark blue chambray, probably left over from a batch of aprons. She wiped a trickle of sweat from her temple, inhaled, and bent over the sewing machine. Her eyelids closed as she slipped the fabric under the presser foot. She toed the pedal on the floor while her fingers moved the cloth under the needle's tooth. Thaya never planned what would be made from a piece of deadstock. Her hands merely guided the material as it transformed itself.

The sounds of the warehouse—a jumble of machines and voices—retreated. Thaya heard the voice of the fabric, its ancestry of individual threads, the field where the fibers were grown. She heard the voices of the women who first wove the fibers into thread, then those who twined the thread into fabric. Thaya could feel the steamy closeness of those other warehouses.

The swatches that she felt strongest were the ones made of animal fibers: sheep wool, yak hair. She could smell the crops they grazed on; feel the cycle of storms and sunshine soaked into their coats.

Human-made swatches were unpleasant to handle and troublesome under the needle. Thaya could sense layers of pollution, the violent methods of extraction. Natural fibers were luxurious but synthetic fabrics were better for the party clothes, winter wear, and other doll fashions that Thaya created: ball gowns for Barbies, superhero capes, Bitsy Baby pajamas.

The chambray in Thaya's hand gave off heavy air molecules, wind, animals. Without knowing why, she sewed two long scraps of facing to each short side of the fabric. She didn't know what the deadstock had turned into until the foreman, a red-headed man with pale hands, appeared beside her. When she looked up from her machine, all the other stations were empty. Through the windows, Thaya saw the streetlights glowing in the dusk.

What is this? the foreman asked.

Thaya handed it to him and realized it was a mask, the kind doctors wore in surgery. She motioned for the foreman to put it on. She frowned. *The ties are too clumsy,* she thought. Thaya pushed out her chair and walked to the remnant wall. She carried a bin of elastic pieces back to her station.

The foreman watched Thaya divide the deadstock into two piles: cotton and everything else. Velvet, chenille, fur, and tulle mask material.

Bring me the rest of the cotton, she told the foreman. *All of it.*

What are we going to do with masks? he asked.

We're getting ready, she said.

Yorba, Yorba

"*Yorba, yorba,*" his aunt yells from the back row of the van we rented for the week. "It's spelled with a J," she says in English, "but said like Y."

I nod but don't turn from the window. I can no longer keep track of what language we are in — Hebrew, Yiddish, Hungarian. Even English sounds foreign at this point. All I know is that we're forever going *yorba* — left. Maybe it's illegal to turn right in Israel.

We're driving to the Dead Sea. All week, David's aunt, uncle, and cousins insisted we must see the Dead Sea. So on the last day of our visit, we set out in the morning from the rocky Mediterranean coast. The dripping bougainvillea reminds me of Southern California as do the green metal highways signs, in English, Hebrew, and Arabic, that use the same font as American ones. After an hour in the car, we see camels and shanty towns more often. We are in the dry, endless desert.

David is driving. His dad, Csaba, rides shotgun, translating when the relatives forget to speak English. I'm in the middle row, sitting between Jacob and Mary to keep them from bickering. They're good kids, but the trip has worn us all down. I let Jacob dissolve into his music while Mary watches a movie. I ignore David's pleas to make the kids look at the scenery.

"They're missing it," he groans.

His dad snorts. "You were the same way. I could hardly get you to look at the Eiffel Tower!"

"This is different."

They rehash — for the hundredth time — the story of their trip to France twenty-five years ago. I close my eyes and try to get comfortable against the low headrest. Behind me, the aunt and uncle speak in Hungarian, the cadence of the language and the warmth of the car pulling me into sleep.

I wake up when the car stops, relieved that we've finally arrived. But we haven't. We're at a checkpoint at the edge of the West Bank. For the first time during our trip, I'm nervous. These young people, with stern faces and machine guns, seem too young to have guns, to be in the military, to point weapons at my children.

I squeeze Mary's hand, not realizing she had slipped hers into mine. I smile tightly as David explains that his uncle had talked to the Israeli soldier in Hebrew so they'd know we were no threat. They wave us through with their guns, the ease of their movements making it more frightening.

"Just two more hours," David announces, trying to be cheerful.

I can't fall back asleep so Mary and I play tic-tac-toe.

David's been to Israel many times with his father since he was a child. It's the first time for me and the kids. I don't know why we waited until now or, honestly, why I have come. We've slept apart for months now. But Csaba invited us. Even though he travels here every year, I cannot believe it's safe. But I couldn't let the children go without me. If something is going to happen to them, I want it to happen to me, too.

I am not foolish enough to think that this trip will change anything. That we will fall back in love and live happily ever after. But I thought we'd find some joy in traveling, like when we were first together.

Long before the kids came, we went to Budapest with Csaba and decided to take the train up to Prague. As we walked to the train station in the rain, a spectacular bolt of lightning struck. We gasped as the sky lit up. Inside, the station was chaos. With David's halting Hungarian, we learned that the lightning torched a track switch, delaying all the trains. We spent eight hours in the cold, grimy station, laughing and talking and kissing. It became one of our favorite memories. But now, there is almost nothing. There have been a few moments, like exploring the market in Jerusalem and seeing the Western Wall, but I know when we return home, what we felt here will be gone.

Finally, we're at the Dead Sea. We crawl out of the van and into the burning sunshine. The parking lot is full of screaming kids, sullen teenagers, parents burdened with coolers and towels. David's aunt and uncle lead us to the water.

As I help Mary down the dirt slope, I see the water and am startled by my disappointment. There are hundreds of people along the water's edge. I can't make them out as individuals, just a mass of sound and motion. Nothing at all like the empty, tranquil beaches boasted about in the travel brochure I read. I turn to David to ask him where that beach is, where we could enjoy the rejuvenation of Dead Sea minerals in solitude like the brochure promised. But David is mediating between his dad and his aunt about where to set up.

On the strip of beach, some of the young women wear bikinis. Others are fully clothed with headscarves. These women are all dark — dark hair, olive skin, flashing brown eyes and attractive in the way that all young women are attractive. My husband could have gone that way. I guess he could still make a beautiful olive-skin child to go with our two redheads.

David and Csaba lead the kids across the rocks and chunks of salt deposits to the water. As he passes by, Csaba asks me something in Hungarian. I guess at what he's saying and answer, "In a minute."

"How do you know what he said?" David calls back.

I shrug and look away. The water is an impossible blue and the sun bores through the useless sunscreen I slather on. My privileged disappointment is tamed by watching our children float in the buoyant water. I'm grateful we're here. Even if they're only half Jewish, even if they don't care about it now, the kids traveled half the world to experience this part of their family history.

I pick my way over the rocks and swim out near the kids. The water is bathtub warm and slick. I taste the salty water and turn to float on my back. Away from the crowd, I feel relief. It's just like every other beach I've been to. Of everything I learned this week, it's that what is true here is true everywhere. Families want to raise their children, observe their religion, have a place of their own. Though that last part is the point of contention here, the undercurrent to every conversation. I ignore the politics. It's not my place to insert myself into this war, something I don't pretend to understand, that I don't feel down to my bones as every family here does.

After floating for a while, I paddle back and sit in the shallow water near the rocks. Nearby are two women in jeans, blouses and headscarves. One woman holds a girl on her lap. The child is about six, her long, wet dress clinging to her body. The child doesn't pay attention to the water and so when a salty wave splashes over them, it hits her open eyes and mouth. She begins to cry.

The women attempt to calm her down, but her crying turns to body-shaking sobs. Everyone on the beach is watching. The child slips away from her mother and runs down the beach. She doesn't look back. The two women chase after her, calling her name. The girl keeps going, as if she'll be safe if she can just get far enough away.

I stand up and shield my eyes against the relentless sun. Soon the girl will run out of beach when the sea meets the rocky cliffs. I hear my own daughter calling my name, but I can't turn my gaze. The girl is almost out of beach but still doesn't slow down. It's as if she's going to run right through solid rock. But I know she'll either have to swim into the water or turn back the way she came.

The Irrational Constant

"You have a fever." Mom loved to point out the obvious. She took her hand from my forehead. "You should stay home."

"I feel fine," I lied.

"You stay up too late with those numbers. I don't know why—"

"Because it's important." I stood up and shouldered my backpack. If I could memorize almost one hundred digits of pi, she could at least remember why I was doing it.

Mom grabbed my arm. "I know it's important. I just don't understand why."

I pulled away, not in the mood to explain it again. Mom's attention could only last a few minutes. Sure enough, when I looked back, her eyes were closed, her mind back to the list in her head.

The List of Never Enough, I called it. At the top was never-enough-money, just edging out never-enough-time. Even though Dad paid child support, Mom said it wasn't the same. Paying for a two-bedroom apartment across town brought us down a tax bracket, Dad tried to explain to me. Later, I asked my brother, Greg, what that meant.

"Such a dipshit," he sneered. "We were lower middle class, now we're officially poor."

I didn't mind patching my backpack with duct tape or not having new clothes. I learned to ignore the teasing a long time ago. What I hated was that everything changed. Mom worked two jobs and was never around. Every other weekend, we stayed with Dad. He exhausted us morning to night with hiking, mini-golf, movies, anything but just hanging out like we used to. I especially hated pinching myself to stay awake on the saggy bottom bunk at his apartment until Greg was asleep. More than once I woke up with a spider crawling on me.

"You should at least wear shorts so you aren't so hot," Mom said.

I ignored her and pulled the front door closed.

Jog-walking to school, I recited the numbers. "Three point four one five…nine two six five three…" Pi was a mathematical constant that had no end. At least, no one had found the end yet. That's what I liked about it. "…five eight nine seven nine…" That the end — the final number — was out there somewhere. Mathematicians had worked at it for centuries and, even though they'd parsed it out to trillions of digits, they still didn't know where it would end. But for all that uncertainty, no matter what size circle was measured, the ratio of circumference to diameter was always, constantly, pi. I explained this to Mom many times. "…three two three eight four…"

I arrived sweaty to first period, having reached eighty-seven digits. Of course I had a fever, but I couldn't miss school. Tomorrow was March 14, the day of the Pi Contest. And, after deducting spring break, Memorial Day, and two teacher in-service days, there were only fifty-seven days until school was out.

I hadn't missed a day all year. This year, the prize for perfect attendance was a trip to Disneyland. Only the few perfect-attendance students and two teachers would go on the last day of school, paid for by the school. Disneyland was only an hour away. Our family used to go for special occasions. The last time was my thirteenth birthday, right before the divorce. Disneyland without my family, especially Greg, would be infinitely better. The bell rang as I walked into History and slid into my seat next to Trae.

"You ready?" Trae asked.

"Think so. I'll get up to ninety-five tonight. That should be enough. I heard Tommy Falgren got—"

"Got to ninety-two, I know." Trae sighed. "Look, Stef and I are going to the mall after school. She said you could come."

"I can't."

"A couple hours at the mall won't hurt." She scowled as Ms. Dennison called for our homework. "You have all night to study."

I shook my head and Trae turned away. She knew I didn't like the mall but never stopped inviting me.

In Math, I finished the in-class assignment quickly and flipped over the paper to write out pi. Mom said I got my love of numbers from her dad. Grandpa lived only a few streets away from school, the same house where Mom grew up, the house where Gramma died. Mom had gone to my high school. Her initials were carved into a locker in the juniors' hallway, but she'd never wanted to come look at it with me.

By the time the lunch bell rang, my head was pounding. I threw up in my mouth a little just looking at the turkey sandwich Mom made. She knew I hated mayonnaise, but half the time forgot. I threw the bag away and walked to the library. I couldn't bear to sit in the hot sun and listen to Trae, Stef, and the others gossip.

I waved to Mrs. Faiges and took a seat at an empty back table. Most days, rather than go home, I studied in the library after school until Mrs. Faiges turned off the lights. She almost always offered me a ride home and could almost always hide the pity on her face.

I laid my head on the table and closed my eyes. When summer came, I'd have to hang out at the public library, which smelled like cooked cabbage. With Dad gone and Mom at work all day, Greg used me as his personal servant, under not-very-vague threats of violence. I wished I could go to a math camp or bring myself to fail a class so I could be assigned summer school. Before the end-of-lunch bell rang, I stopped by the desk to tell Mrs. Faiges I wouldn't be staying after school.

"You look like you should go home now," she said.

"I know."

"Here." She scribbled on a piece of paper and handed it to me. "Go see the nurse."

The nurse waved away the paper I offered. "Don't need that to know you should go home," she said.

"Could I just stay here for a little while? Maybe I'll feel better." I lay down on the cot.

"I'm calling your mother."

"No." I reached out to her. "I have perfect attendance."

"You're sick."

"Please."

She sighed and let go. "Let me ask the attendance office how many periods count as a school day."

I curled up on the cot as she turned off the light and closed the door. The hallway outside quieted as students disappeared into classrooms.

If today counted as attendance, I could walk to Grandpa's instead of going home. I could nap on his couch and then study my numbers. He'd order us a pizza and drive me home just before bedtime. I would feel better tomorrow and beat Tommy Falgren by at least two numbers. If today counted, I'd have perfect attendance and go to Disneyland. I closed my eyes and waited for the nurse to return.

The Place We Held Our Wedding is Now a Surf Shop

I'm not sentimental, but I don't want to be erased. That's why I motion the salesperson over to the table of folded green and yellow T-shirts. This is where we cut the cake, I explain.

She narrows her eyes, trying, I can tell, to decide if I'm a well-dressed weirdo or a Vicodin-addled housewife, and which one might cause more trouble. The ceremony was at the church on the hill, I continue, but we had the reception here.

Recognition in her eyes. She waves me over to a wall with framed black and white photos. The third from the left is what it looked like when we got married, though I remember the day in bright colors. Twenty-five years ago; the lifetime of the young woman beside me.

I move toward the curved wall of windows where two hundred guests enjoyed chicken or lasagna in green-leathered booths. I trace the steps we took, newly minted and naive, handing out lace bags of sugared almonds as wedding favors.

Our divorce was drama-free, just like our marriage, but the wedding was as magical as a little girl's dream. The voluminous dress is packed in a shadow box in the attic, too luckless to give away. The beloved shoes, I dyed black and sold at a tag sale.

I pluck a pair of sunglasses from the display that stands where the band played love songs. $16.95. Tourist pricing, I think, as I search for cash in my purse. The salesgirl cuts the tag and I wear the sunglasses out into the bright sun, passing the surfboards that stand where we once danced.

Quesadillas at Midnight

I don't hear the garage door open, so when my daughter slumps into the kitchen at midnight with her faded duffel bag, I'm startled. The water glass slips from my hand and shatters on the tile floor. Pete the Pug rushes in, still half asleep. I grab his collar, lifting him before he reaches any of the pieces shimmering in the moonlight through the window.

My daughter pulls the broom and dustpan from the pantry. I kneel to help, with Pete on my hip like I used to hold my daughter in this kitchen. I don't question her surprise visit from college and she doesn't offer anything. Is it a boy—a girl?—or academics or simply the exhaustion that comes with making all of your own decisions.

I'm standing at the sink in the kitchen because I woke up thirsty from the mask of the sleep apnea machine. I'm supposed to keep my mouth closed when I sleep so that the air pumps through my nose but inevitably, when I'm deep down into sleep, my jaw relaxes and my mouth opens. Any moisture is whisked away and I wake up gagging.

When we've swept up all the glass, I offer to make quesadillas, the greasy kind I make when one of us needs comforting. She nods and sits cross-legged on a kitchen chair with Pete. He's really too big for her lap, but soon he's asleep.

From a drawer in the refrigerator, I grab a pack of corn tortillas and a chunk of Colby Jack. My daughter is quiet against the dog's snoring. When she was younger, she used to drown me with her stories and dreams; her joy and sadness overwhelming me at times. During the months she's at school, I long for the noise and chaos of those days.

I grate the cheese and heat oil in the pan. She sets the dog on the floor and washes up at the sink. We stand over our assembly line of cheese, tortillas and hot oil, and take turns stacking quesadillas on a plate. Not waiting for them to cool, we burn our tongues on the first crispy bite. I know her words will flow soon but for now, eating together in silence is enough.

Worry, Incorporated

As soon as she stepped into the lobby of the Tranquility office, Melody was knocked over by a skinny bald man in a navy tracksuit. She landed on the floor, her purse upended and one wedge sandal knocked off, but the man didn't stop or apologize. He disappeared down the hallway to her left.

"Sorry about that." A woman in a tan pantsuit rushed over. "Not a good start to your first day."

As Melody righted herself, she noticed two parallel strips of masking tape on the carpet from one end of the lobby to the other. She started to ask about it when the woman handed Melody her shoe.

"I'm Olivia. We spoke on the phone. You alright?"

Melody slid on her shoe. She was more annoyed than anything. "Who was that?"

"Joe. Doesn't stop for anything." She helped Melody to her feet. "And that's Devon." Olivia gestured to the young Black man on the phone at the large front desk. His pinstriped suit, including a pink pocket square, was out of place among the muted beige walls and carpet. He waved at Melody. "Whatever you need," Oliva continued, "he knows everything. Come this way."

Olivia led Melody around the wall behind the receptionist desk where there was a bank of lockers, a refrigerator and a countertop with coffee pots and snacks. "Help yourself to coffee, then choose a locker."

Melody set down her purse and selected a mug and Keurig pod.

"In the morning, leave your belongings in a locker." She gestured to the wall. "Be sure to write down your combination—"

"I don't have an office?" Melody interrupted as the coffee finished brewing.

"Dubbers don't have offices."

"Dubbers?"

"Worriers. Double u. Dubbers. That's what you're called."

With her monochrome suit and vaguely disconcerting manner, Olivia reminded Melody of a neighbor from her childhood. The woman hosted direct sales parties for makeup or kitchen gadgets that Melody attended with her mom. Melody didn't know why they didn't just go to Target. Melody's dad called it a scam.

What did I get myself into? Melody thought. The job description had been vague but she needed a job.

"Anyway, lockers, coffee, then choose the environment you want to work in. There," Olivia gestured to a monitor on the wall, "you can see which rooms are open. Use the tablet on the table to sign one out. It'll make more sense when you see the rooms."

Joe came into the kitchen from the other end of the hallway. "Break time," he said as he grabbed a granola bar. "I'm sorry I ran over you," he said to Melody. "You okay?"

"More surprised than anything," she said.

"Welcome to Worry, Incorporated," he replied with a smile.

"Joe can't sit still," Olivia said after he left. "He taped his own track on the hallway ringing the building—about a mile all the way around."

"He just walks all day?" Melody asked.

Olivia nodded. "He handles mainly self-esteem issues. Steady work, there. Most of our work comes from clients who can't sleep because of their worries. Or repeat clients who don't have the time—or energy—to worry about things that can't be fixed. That's the point. Research shows that worrying's done by a part of the brain that doesn't respond to reason or evidence. By letting us worry for them, they have more time and energy to live a better life."

"Like how I worry about what my mother will say when I get a new haircut?" Melody asked.

"Precisely. Outsource that worry to us—like dropping off your dry cleaning. Except you never need to pick it back up."

Melody wondered if it really was that easy. She'd tried everything to stop her mind from racing when she went to bed at night: warm milk, deep breathing, journaling. She had to read boring history books or biographies, sometimes for hours, until she couldn't keep her eyes open.

At the beginning of the outer hallway, Olivia stopped to make sure Joe wasn't coming. She gestured to the doors and windows down the hall. "Each room has a theme. You can sit in the same room all day, every day, or move around. Whatever helps you do your best worrying."

Olivia pointed to a window on the right. Melody peered into the small, low-lit room with powder blue walls, a wooden rocking chair and a desk with a three-ring binder, pencil, and legal pad on it. A young woman with long dark hair placed a ticking white kitchen timer on the desk. Then she picked up a green blanket from the floor, sat down in the chair and started rocking furiously.

"Lailani specializes in family and children," Olivia said, "especially pregnancies, adoption, and separation anxiety. She's the queen of kindergarten."

"Will I specialize?" Melody asked.

"If you want. Or you can be a generalist. We always need both. But you don't need to decide for a while."

In another room, a small, middle-aged woman was curled up on the edge of a sofa with a box of tissues. Olivia explained that Catherine took on lonely-heart and tortured-artist cases.

"Her specialty is the sensitive soul," Olivia said.

Melody watched the woman twist with sobs. "I can't fake cry for anyone," she said.

"We don't want you to fake anything. Everyone worries in their own way."

At a room two doors down, the window didn't have a curtain but it was still difficult to see inside. When her eyes adjusted, Melody saw that it was decorated like an old man's study: dark wood paneling, dark furniture, and a fake fireplace. She could just make out a man with gray hair sitting in a club chair.

"Harold," Olivia said as the man lifted a pipe to his mouth. "It's not lit. He just gnaws on it."

Melody nodded and they started walking again. Finally, Olivia stopped at an open door with a sign above that read "Soft." Inside, the floor had wall-to-wall carpet and the four walls were covered in fabric of different colors and textures. The desk held a binder, pencil, legal pad, and kitchen timer. A soft chair facing the window looked big enough for two people.

"Like I said on the phone, we'll start you off with a thirty-day trial period," Olivia said. "If you don't like it, well, no harm done, right?" They stepped inside. "I reserved this room for you," Olivia continued, "and here's your binder. There's a variety of cases. You can work them in any order you like, so long as you finish at least ten a day. Time management, that's the key. You have, for instance," she skimmed the first case, "Sam, who's a sophomore in high school and worried about his midterm exam." She turned the page. "Then there's Harriet. Worried her husband'll leave her and her dog'll die. You can probably give fifteen minutes to Sam. Harriet needs at least thirty, maybe forty-five."

"So I set the timer for each?" Melody asked.

"Bingo." Olivia flipped to the front sheet. "Next to each name, write how much time you spent worrying and any follow-up needed. You know, a half hour or two more hours. We charge by fifteen-minute increments, so the more they need, the better it is for business. At the end of the day, turn your binder and sheet in to Devon. Pick up your binder and new sheet the next morning. He's working to computerize the system but we're not there yet."

Melody glanced through the binder sections: Career, Children, Dating, Death, Health, Holidays, Marriage, Money, Parents, Pets, and Other. Even if it was a scam, it was still a lot of work. And she'd quit worse jobs.

"So what do you think?"

Melody nodded. "I'll give it a try."

After Olivia left, Melody read a brochure about the history of Tranquility, then thumbed through a few cases. After writing out some thoughts about Sam, Melody set the timer and sat down. She worried about all the things that could go wrong during a high school midterm exam. Once in a while Joe walked by, hands clasped behind his back. When the timer went off, Melody set it again for Harriet.

The next morning, Melody watched for Joe as she opened the office door. She talked to Devon for a few minutes, then signed out a room. Inside the Quilt Room, Melody slid off her sandals to dig her toes into the plush carpeting. She studied the elaborate quilts on the walls, then settled into the soft recliner.

Flipping through the binder, she settled on a case from a mother, Patrice, afraid her daughter was marrying the wrong man. He was telling her what to think, how to act, how to dress. The mother was worried. Melody leaned against the headrest and closed her eyes.

There was a knock on the door; Melody opened her eyes. The binder was on the floor. She forgot to set the timer and, looking at her watch, had slept for four hours. She'd have to pick a less comfortable room next time. The door opened.

"Hi!" It was the woman with dark hair. "Olivia wanted me to check on you. I'm Lailani."

"The rocking chair room." Melody picked up the binder. "That's me. Want to stretch your legs?"

As they walked through the hallways, Lailani offered commentary on her favorite rooms—Knitting, Lego, Squeeze Balls—while Melody peeked into a few that didn't have the curtain drawn. Olivia was right, everyone worried in a different way: an old woman kissing a rosary; a young man sitting on the floor with his head in his hands; a grown woman sprawled on a mattress on the floor, throwing a tantrum like an overtired three-year-old.

"I'm pretty sure my new case is Devon," Lailani said. "What?"

"Devon, at the front desk. I think the reason he overdresses is that—"

"Please." Melody shook her head. "I don't want to know what he worries about."

"Ok, well, then I probably shouldn't tell you that if you get a case about the LSATs, that's me."

"Why would you tell me that?" Melody groaned. Then curiosity won out. "Wait, you submit your own worries? And you're taking the LSATs?"

"This is just to get me through the last year of undergrad. And why wouldn't I want someone to worry for me? We get a discount. You should try it."

"You believe it works?"

"I don't have any evidence that says it doesn't."

"Come on," Melody said. "You can't prove a negative."

Lailani laughed. "You'd make a good lawyer."

"Who's that?" Melody stopped short at a room at the very back of the building.

Inside the undecorated room, a woman with long, braided hair relaxed on a yellow couch reading a paperback, no timer or binder in sight. The woman looked up and caught Melody's eye. She smirked, then returned to the book.

"Ruth. She's the founder's granddaughter. Ignore her."

"What's her specialty?"

"Doing whatever she wants."

"She just reads all day?"

Lailani groaned. "I don't want to talk about Ruth. Come on, I'll take you to my favorite deli for lunch. We can walk there."

By the end of her third week at Tranquility, Melody had settled in and told Olivia she would stay. She was still skeptical, but if people believed in it enough to email their worries to strangers, then she might as well do her job.

One day, as she walked to get her lunch from the fridge, Melody saw Ruth walking toward the back door. Melody grabbed her purse from the locker and hurried down the hallway after her.

"Excuse me!" she called as Ruth crossed the parking lot, heading toward a row of pine trees. Ruth didn't turn around so Melody jogged to catch up. "Sorry to bother you."

"Then don't," Ruth said without turning around.

"You're Ruth, right?" Melody stammered. "I'm Melody. I'm new."

"Congratulations."

Melody followed Ruth along a path through the trees. "Could I ask you something?"

"If I said no, would that stop you?" They walked in silence over the railroad tracks and along a service road to a strip mall. Ruth stopped at the entrance to a diner. "If you want to ask questions, you're paying."

They sat in a booth at the back of the restaurant. Between the braids, the childish overalls and laugh lines, Ruth's age was anyone's guess.

"I already know what you're going to ask," Ruth said.

"What?"

"Why do I just read books all day?"

"Is it because you can't get fired?"

"No. And here's my question." Ruth leaned across the table. "Why do you care? Or are you another busybody like Lailani?"

"I don't mean—" Melody was interrupted by the waiter putting down water glasses. "I just wonder, why even come to the office if you don't work the cases?"

"Because it doesn't matter."

"Worrying for our clients doesn't matter?"

A waiter appeared and took their order.

"What did you learn from reading the company history?" Ruth asked when he left.

"Your great-grandfather started a soap company. Somehow your grandfather turned that into Tranquility."

"Do you remember the name?"

"Of the soap? Grand Savon?"

"Very good. Grand Savon—fat soap. My great-grandmother came up with the name. It was a soap to help you lose weight."

"Soap can't help you lose weight."

The waiter set down their plates.

"Do you want to hear the story or not?" Ruth snapped, making the waiter flinch.

Melody sighed and nodded. Ruth ate slowly, wiping her mouth after every bite. She loved an audience, Melody thought, though she probably seldom had one.

"They opened a storefront on Main Street in Kansas City around 1920. They couldn't make the soap fast enough. He was one of the country's first millionaires. Not affected by the crash at all. They were selling soap but that's not what people were buying. What were they buying, really?"

Melody thought for a minute. "A lie?"

"Wrong." Ruth shook her head. "Hope. My great-grandfather was selling hope. His son, my grandfather, wanted to be an actor. After his dad died, he sold the business and moved to LA. But he wasn't a good actor and ended up helping to start Scientology."

"That wasn't in the brochure."

"I tried to put it in the brochure, but the lawyers killed it."

"Go on, then."

"My grandfather didn't stay with Scientology long, though. But it reinforced how much people were willing to pay for hope. So he started Tranquility."

"You think Tranquility is another Scientology?"

"Kind of. But not a cult."

"But it's a scam. And that's why you take a paycheck but don't do the work."

"Oh, it's not a scam," Ruth said. "It works."

"How can you possibly know that?" Melody signaled for the check.

"Because I'm the placebo. I don't do any worrying and my repeat and non-repeat client rates are exactly the same as everybody else's."

"Then what's the point of Tranquility? Besides taking people's money?"

"Don't you see?" Ruth leaned across the table. "It's the existence of Tranquility that matters. And the simple act of paying for it. Most people don't believe in the power of prayer because they're skeptical that something free could work. But because they pay us to worry, they believe it works. The more worries they unload onto us, the better they feel—like they're getting their money's worth. Whether we actually worry or not is irrelevant."

"That seems…Why didn't Olivia tell me any of that?"

"It's just business for her. A job. I don't know what she believes." She stood up from the table. "And I don't care. But, hey, thanks for lunch."

Melody paid the bill and sat by herself for a few minutes, wondering if she could believe any part of Ruth's story.

A few months later, Melody sat cross-legged on the couch in the Puzzle Room after lunch and reviewed Sam's latest intake sheet. His grades were up but prom was coming and he was afraid of rejection no matter who he asked.

Despite what Ruth had said, Melody believed she was helping her clients. On her own time, she also worried about Lailani and her LSATs. Her own sleep hadn't improved so she submitted a few of her own worries. It couldn't hurt.

Melody set the timer. She imagined Sam, Harriet, Lailani, and the others hiking up a snowy mountain. Every few steps, they let something slip to the ground—a backpack, water bottle, coat. They were letting go as they climbed, not so they could find their way back down but so that when they reached the top, they were light enough to fly.

Acknowledgements

First, "thank you" isn't enough to convey my gratitude to Michele McDannold and Roadside Press for publishing this collection of stories. Your fierce support of odd, weird, and absurd literature is a rebellious island in a sea of mediocrity.

To the many journals that published these stories individually, thank you for giving them a home in the world.

Thank you to the Greater Columbus Arts Council for championing artists in Central Ohio and supporting me with multiple grants while I wrote the stories in this book.

My everlasting love and appreciation for Clockhouse Writers' Conference and all the talented writers who offered feedback, words of support, and hugs over the years, especially Lucy Turner, Lucinda Garthwaite, David Waite, Julie Parent, Ken Damerow, Maureen Dunphy, Carolyn Locke, Chrystal Wing, Tracy Roberts, Jeff Ihlenfeldt, Janna Sakson, Cass Winner, Sarah Shellow, Sam Sherman, Darlene Olivo, Kathryn Cullen-DuPont, Trish Shepherd, and Jeff Eisenbrey.

Thank you, Matthew and Garrett, for your understanding and love. For their constant encouragement, thank you to my parents, Joan and Ned, and my parents-in-law, Shirlee and Ted.

Most of all, thank you to my husband, Dan. I never thought I could write a story. Or get one published. Or publish a book. Here I am now with two books. I could not have done it without your unwavering love, support, and belief in me—especially when I didn't believe in myself.

Grateful acknowledgement is made to where these pieces were previously published:

Last Bus to Stonehenge, *Bridge Eight*
The Wrong Way, *Paragraph Planet*
The Best One-Armed Waiter in the West, *Sequestrum*
All the Kids Are in Therapy, *The Good Life Review*
Current Disasters, *October Hill*
Not the Worst Day of Your Life but Definitely Not the
    Best, *The Harpoon Review*
The Milkbone Deposition, *Dragon Boat Review*
We Always Break Up Near Water, *Burningword Literary
    Journal*
The Jumping-Off Point, *Santa Fe Literary Review*
American Gothic Getaway, *Doubleback Review*
Family Vacation Dictionary, *the tiny journal*
The Uncluded, *The Oddville Press*
Stuffed Peppers to Please Everybody, *Does It Have Pockets?*
The Poles of Inaccessibility, *Flint Hills Review*
Her Boyfriend with the Difficult Name, *Sledgehammer Lit*
The Other Side of Luck, *Red Rock Review*
Deadstock, *Reflex Press*
Yorba, Yorba, *The Bookends Review*
The Irrational Constant, *The Louisville Review*
The Place We Held Our Wedding is Now a Surf Shop, *The
    Disappointed Housewife*
Quesadillas at Midnight, *Tiny Moments Anthology Vol. 5,*
    Bronze Bird Books
Worry, Incorporated, *Hindsight*

Jen McConnell has published prose and poetry in more than forty literary magazines and her work has been nominated twice for a Pushcart Prize. She received her MFA from Goddard College. Her first story collection, *Welcome, Anybody*, was published by Press 53. She currently serves as the publisher of *CLOCKHOUSE* Journal. A California native, she's lived in the Midwest long enough that she should be used to the winters by now.

More Roadside Press Titles

9 798990 546691